Love Found Me

By
Vanessa Richardson

"Love Found Me"

Published by
GSH Publishing
P. O. Box 350646
Palm Coast, FL 32135

Copyright © 2009 by Vanessa Richardson
www.gshpublishing.com

This book is a work of fiction.

Library of Congress Cataloging-in-Publication Data

Library of Congress Control Number:
2009940559

ISBN: 9780615334530

Printed in the United States of America

Acknowledgements

I would like express my heartfelt gratitude to my mother, Rosa Meredith, who continually supports me in all my endeavors no matter how strange or impossible they may seem. Her strength and belief in me are what galvanize me to continue through my ups and downs. Without her guidance and encouragement in me, my accomplishments would have been next to impossible.

Thank you to my wonderful Elder Meredith. Your word deposits have drawn interest. To my buddy—Johnnie (Rabbit) Chestnutt. I can still hear your prayers ringing in my ears. You are missed.

I would like to thank my wonderful church family Deliverance Victory Temple Ministries, for your staid support of me. It means the world to me. I am grateful to my wonderful sisters and brothers; for believing in me, you always have my back in my "ouch" days. I love you guys. To Patricia and Robin, my PR ladies. Thank you so much! Word of mouth is the best of advertisements.

To the Sisters, thank you for your prayers and words of encouragement. They are hidden in my heart never to be forgotten. To all my wonderful cast members of every stage production I performed. The best is yet to come! I love you and thank you! Thank you to GSH Publishing, you guys rocks! If I have forgotten anyone, please blame my head and not my heart. You are appreciated!

Love Found Me

VANESSA RICHARDSON

Prologue

Thick, dark, ominous clouds blotted out the moon, occasionally casting the world into an eerie darkness. The last blackout was many, many years ago. Fate would have it that this night would be a repeat of history. Below, the streets were empty, not even a drunkard could be found on the barren streets. Out of fear, many sought the comfort and safety of their homes.

The house was quiet, for now anyway, but she was not fooled. Never would she play the fool again. Rocking back and forth, she waited patiently and was not disappointed. It was all one sick routine. The whimpering began, followed by the squeaking of the old mattress and then, thump...thump...thump.

Thump. "I hate you!" Thump. "I hate you!" Thump. "I hate you!" Her words matched the thumps in song, powerful words for a ten-year-old. Words a ten-year-old should never have to say and mean. Then again, she was not an average ten-year-old, as she had endured and seen too much.

Something was not right. The routine was off tonight. Her breathing quicken with fear. Chills began to form on her arms, and the hairs at the nape of her neck standing at attendance gave testament that something was not right.

Scurrying from the worn mattress, the child peeked through the door, being careful not to make any noise as she stepped out into the dark hallway. She knew the old house well...too well. She was forbidden to leave the dilapidated house, not even to attend school. She and her mother were both prisoners, had been so for the last six years. Her father thought the outside world was toxic, and didn't want her and her mother to become stained by their ignorance.

Instincts screamed for her to seek safety. It would be so easy for her to climb out her bedroom window and leave. Nevertheless, she could not leave her mother. Warm tears began to course down the child's cheek, springing from sad, beautiful eyes. Eyes that

1

should have witnessed the good that life had to offer. She knew that crying was useless, yet she could not stop their flow.

Glancing back out of the bedroom window, her heart plummeted. She desperately wanted to leave. Every nerve ending prompted her to do so.

"I can't leave Mama," she whispered to her constant companion. Unfolding her tiny hands, a small onyx button winked at her, remaining silent. The button was from a doll her mother had given her when she was three years old. She would pretend the doll was her sister.

The doll had curly brown hair, two black button eyes, and a wide smile. That was what she loved most about her sister doll, her smile. She herself never smiled. She didn't have a reason to. Her world was devoid of smiles and laughter because of him. She was deathly afraid of him.

She dare not say his name aloud, to think it brought fear upon her. She simply referred to him as him. He was a tall and robust man with a receding hairline. Nothing about him stood out in particular but his eyes. She had never seen such eyes like his before, but she tried not to look into them because they were terrifying. They weren't a coffee-brown color, as her mother and her eyes were, his were popped-eyed black and lifeless. They reminded her of the fish Mama would oftentimes cook for him. When he addressed Mama, she would always keep her head down. He didn't mind this; she sensed her subservient attitude gave him a feeling of power.

Her father was a janitor at a local catholic school, and would often come home complaining about the hypocrites, and how one day true dominance would reign; a doctrine that a six-year-old knew nothing about.

Her father was a creature of habit. Everyday, at precisely 6:30 pm, Mama had to have his supper cooked and placed in front of his favorite recliner next to his remote. One day Mama was not feeling well, and had slept restlessly all day.

"Baby, come here," her mother said.

Immediately, she went to her mother, crawling in bed next to her. Her mother hugged her tightly, gently caressing her cheek. "Mommy is not feeling good. So, you have to be a big girl and fix yourself something to eat. When the mailman comes, let Mommy know so she can get up and fix Daddy's supper, okay?" The mailman always arrived before her dad arrived home.

"Yes, Mommy, I can do it, I'm a big girl." The little girl kissed her mother's gaunt cheek, and was surprised by how hot her skin felt.

She would do something her mother couldn't do...protect her. With her sister doll in her hand; she went into the kitchen, dragged out one of the chairs; and placed it in front of the living room window. There she waited. She never did fix herself a sandwich, she was too afraid she would miss the mailman's arrival. Her bladder was full, but she refused to abandon her watch.

"I am so hungry," she told her sister doll. "You are too? It won't be long now. Mama will fix us something to eat soon." She remembered the leftover spaghetti from last night, and immediately her stomach growled loudly.

The sound of someone whistling caught her attention. It was the mailman. She immediately went to tell her mama. However, her mother wouldn't get up, she was so hot. She decided to let her rest longer. That was a decision she would forever regret.

Papa came home and was outraged that his meal was not prepared. He went into a raging frenzy. He grabbed Mama by the arms, screaming such horrid and explicit words. Mama weakly apologized, trying to explain to him how sick she was.

At first, she thought her father would do physical harm to her mother, but he must have felt how hot her mother's skin was because he pulled his hand back quickly, rubbing it on one of his pants leg, and said, "Go lie down. I'm going into town to get me something to eat." He left muttering under his breath something about lazy women and children. Mama was never late with his meals again.

One day when she was six years old the routine changed.

"Let her get my meal and drink." Papa was in one of his cat and mouse games. This was when he was feeling playful. He didn't yell or scream; he simply watched you with his evil eyes. She would rather he yell and scream. Those moments didn't last long. The cat and mouse games were long and intimidating.

Mama laughed nervously. "She is too small, she might drop it. I'll get it. I made your favorite tonight…spaghetti." Mama turned to go into the kitchen.

Papa swore loudly, and one hand snaked out, stopping her. "I said let her do it. The little dirt bag needs to learn some responsibility around here. Eating up all my food and doing nothing. I'm not raising a lazy child. If she is the one, she will understand the responsibilities that are required of her." Her mother stood there, ringing her hands nervously.

She stood there, waiting for a signal from her mother. Her heart was pounding so hard she feared it was going to explode inside of her. Her mother nodded, offering her a paltry smile. She took no comfort in the smile, she was not fooled. She saw the stark fear in her mother's eyes, but returned the smile to Mama.

She was a big girl; she could get her father's meal. She had seen her mother do it a thousand times. When her father came home, she knew what to do, however fear was causing her hands to shake uncontrollably. Successfully, she gave him his huge plate of spaghetti. He just watched her with his popped-eyes. Shivering, she fearfully went into the kitchen for his beverage. She wrapped both hands around the glass of beer, walking tentatively toward her father. The smell of the beer was making her allergies flare up, causing her to sneeze. The beer spilled onto her father's faded pants. Outraged, he stood abruptly, shoving her roughly to the floor, calling her several choice words, some she recognized, others she didn't.

Hand raised, her father advanced upon her, and she shrieked aloud in fear. She back paddled until she reached the wall. He knelt down eye level with her. She was so scared she could hardly breathe. She could only shake her head from side to side, wanting to beg for forgiveness. Fear caused the words to lodge in her throat, and her large coffee-brown eyes pooled with tears. Her father suddenly paused. Slowly, he lowered his hand.

"You little piss ant. If it were up to me, you would've been gone a long time ago." He eyed her with disgust. "What is it about you that they need you?"

She raised her brows in confusion. *They? Who were they? What was he talking about?* She looked at her mother for help. Her mother's only response was to hold her head down. There would be no help coming from her...again. That was when it happened. Something inside her died. She wanted to hate her mother, but found she could not. It was obligation that kept her by her mother's side, that and the fact that she had nowhere else to go.

"Your mother could not do it, what made them think her tainted spawn would be able to do it," her father said.

The child's eyes were wild with fear; tears began to pool in them. For a moment her father's eyes softened, only to harden again. He stood staring down at her.

"I will teach you to stop wasting good beer," he said. He strode angrily into her room, returning with her sister doll in his hand. Shaking the doll, her father laughed maniacally. Her mother slid silently to the living room floor, drawing her knees up, rocking back and forth. Screaming profanities, her father yelled, "This is what happens to bad little girls." He then proceeded to slap the doll until its head fell over, rolling next to her feet.

Her father's voice seemed far away. Her head was pounding painfully. Yet, not once did her eyes leave her sister doll, who was still smiling. If her doll could smile through trouble, then she could too.

Gasping in shock, the child noticed one of the doll's button eyes was missing. She reached out her hands for her doll. Slapping her hand away, her father walked to the kitchen, threw the doll into the sink, and poured cooking oil on the doll. He lit a match, successfully burning the doll.

She followed her father into the kitchen, watching the

yellow-red flames eat away at her sister doll. It was too much. Leaping up screaming, she charged her father with as much force as her tiny body would allow her. He turned in surprise. She briefly remembered feeling a moment of triumph at his look, before connecting with his body. Detached, she watched as he toppled over one of the kitchen table chairs, landing hard. He looked up at her in wide- eyed surprise. Taking advantage of his shock, she kicked him as hard as she could in his private part. This was a lesson learned from her mama.

Her father let out a loud scream that made her cover her ears. She could hear someone else screaming. The sound was powerfully frightening. Her father must have heard it too, as he stopped his whimpering and was staring at her. It finally registered that the screams where coming from her. How long she stood there screaming, she may never know.

When it was over, she slumped to the kitchen floor, feeling empty. She murmured repetitively, "She was my sister. She was my sister."

This must have appeased her father's anger. With a smirk, he turned and went back to his favorite brown recliner in the living room. Mama silently got up off the floor, and in minutes reappeared with a fresh can of beer. She fluffed his pillows, placed his feet on the coffee table, and turned and walked back into the kitchen. She began to clean the mess her father made.

Sometime later, Mama bent down and picked up her sleeping daughter from where she had cried herself to sleep. Placing her child on the worn mattress, she bent down and kissed her. The child opened her eyes and smiled at her mama.

"She was my sister. She was my sister," the child said. Mama said not a word.

Undressing her daughter for bed, she just smiled. She then opened her daughter's hand, and placed a black button in the palm of her hand. The child's heart accelerated. She had a piece of her sister with her. She hugged her mama and smiled. Mama pulled back the covers, and the child slid into the bed with her button held firmly in her little hand, pulling the covers over her. Tears silently falling, her Mama silently kissed her cheek.

After a few restless moments, the child finally slept, dreaming of a place where little girls like her played all day. No one could hurt them there. There were no tears or fears, just happiness.

Shrugging the memory off, the child whispered, "I won't leave her. I'm all she has."

A little while later, a loud crash caused the child to jump. Fear paralyzed her. The palms of her hands were beginning to sweat. The noise did not come from the bedroom. It came from downstairs. She could hear rapid sounds of whispering. Forcing her feet into obedience, she moved toward the stairs. The lights were out. Taking one last regretful look at the window, she descended the stairs, still mindful of the creaks in the old wood floors. The muffled voices continued. The rapid fall of sweat was irritating her eyes, and her throat was dry from fear. She swiped angrily at the fast forming perspiration. *Stay to the shadows child.* The voice! Normally, she would have ignored the voice out of fear. Not tonight. Tonight, she embraced it.

Her mother was the only one who knew about the voice. She dared not mention it to anyone else, as she was forbidden to do so. Mama told her that people would take her to some bad place if she ever told anyone.

It is time, child. Even the voice seemed different tonight. Time for what? Where was Mama? Reaching the landing, the child stayed in the shadows. The door stood ajar. The brisk October wind caused her to shiver and her teeth to chatter. Someone had lit several candles; the dim light gave the room a haunted look. The whispering grew frantic, and it was coming from the kitchen.

Everything happened so fast, it was all a blur. She was flung across the room, hitting her head on the old table. The pain was blinding. She felt something warm and sticky running down her face. She touched her head, and was shocked to see blood on her hand. Her stomach began to rebel. She took a deep breath to keep from fainting.

She heard her mother's screams and then felt her familiar embrace.

"Leave her alone, you monsters!" her mother screamed wildly.

She had never heard her mother scream before. Even when Papa screamed at her or manhandled her, she remained silent. This was indicative of the seriousness of the situation.

The fast falling blood made vision difficult for the child. She tried to comfort Mama, but the words refused to be released.

"We don't have any money. Take what is here, just leave us alone, please!" her mother pleaded. *This is all my fault*, Mama thought. *If only I had left when I had the chance. Now my only child may die. God, please help us. Give us another chance.* "Look what you have done. I have got to get her to a hospital or she will die."

The dark figure only laughed at her pitiful plea. Angry steps followed her cry for help. The child whimpered when she felt the separation of her mother's embrace.

Hard slapping sounds reverberated in the small room. Her mother's screams followed suit. The child tried again to call out to her mother, but lacked the energy.

"Dear God! What do you want from us?"

The intruders' voices were muffled by the black masks they wore. One of the deviants stepped forward; his movements were sure and confident, as if he had all the time in the world. Roughly pulling the woman to her feet, he slapped her twice before throwing her against the wall. She fell like a rag doll. Her mother looked at him in fear, searching his eyes for a small sign of mercy. The dark mask and clothing made him look menacing. He held her stare, angling his head to the side, he smiled sinisterly. She knew then that there would be no mercy coming from him.

"Don't speak unless spoken to. It's not about money, breeder. It's about The New World Order. And your God has nothing to do with it or you, breeder," the masked man, who had slapped her mother, replied. She assumed he was the leader. He was a foot taller than the others.

"Sir, we looked all over the house. He isn't here," a voice interrupted.

The tall masked man answered, "I didn't think he would be. He knows his time is up. So he ran like the coward he is. The Triune won't be pleased by this. You know what to do. Do it quickly."

"Yes sir."

The child rapidly blinked her eyes, trying desperately to see. Where was her father? Why was the bad man hitting her mother? Darkness was creeping in, she wanted to yield to it, but knew she could not. Everything in her screamed at her to stay awake. The blood was still oozing fast, making it hard for her to see. Her limbs refused to obey her command to move.

She could hear her mother screaming again, only this time it sounded different. Clothing could be heard ripping. The child's stomach heaved, and last night's dinner surfaced. She continued to heave long after her stomach emptied its contents. She could hardly catch her breath. *This must be what it feels like to die*, she thought.

I am with you, child. The voice! She never talked to the voice. She was always afraid to, but they were in trouble and Mama needed help. Suppressing her fear, she answered the voice. *Please help my mother. Help us, please!* Silence. Was the voice angry at her for never answering?

Her head was hurting terribly. She could no longer keep the darkness at bay. The room began to shrink. Mama's frantic wailing was becoming faint. Then finally…blessed darkness.

LOVE FOUND ME

Chapter 1

The storm was intense that night. The sharp sound of thunder filled the air. Rain was falling ruthlessly from the dark sky. The howling wind was beating mercilessly against the windowpane. Challenging man and animals alike, forcing them to seek refuge from its fury. Veins of lightning lit the sky.

None of these happenings bothered him. Like a silent centurion, he stood there gazing out his bedroom window, seeing but not seeing. He was no longer afraid of storms. They intrigued him. Tonight he was restless and could not sleep. Sliding his glass door open, he walked out onto the terrace. Immediately, he was drenched by the fast falling rain.

It became a routine. In the wee hours of the morning, he would get up, stare out the window, and remember. He would always remember. His insomnia had been a thorn in his side since moving back home. At first, he chalked it up to nervous energy.

He would be starting a new job soon. He just moved into a new home. He was nervous about seeing old friends again, and the questions they were surely going to ask him. Mike closed his eyes and groaned.

"Maybe it was a mistake returning here." He lifted his head up to the sky. The raindrops felt cool against his skin. Hearing his phone ring caused him to smile. He reentered his bedroom, unmindful of the water trail he was creating. He answered on the third ring.

"What's up, Bryan," he said, already knowing who it was.

His brother laughed. "How did you know it was me?"

Glancing at his watch, Mike smiled. "Bryan, only you would dare call me at 2 o'clock in the morning."

"That's because I'm your twin. So I have certain privileges." There was a small pause. "Are you alright, man?" Bryan asked worriedly.

"I'm fine. Look, old man, get yourself some sleep and enjoy

your beautiful wife and new babies." His brother had just recently become a father to fraternal twins; a girl and boy. "That is where your focus should be," Mike lovingly chastised.

Bryan refused to be derailed. "Mike, I'm serious. Are you alright, man?"

Mike should have known he would never be able to fool his brother. It was hard for either of them to hide their true feelings from each other. Mike often heard that identical twins shared a unique connection with each other. He believed that, as he and Bryan would often sense when something was wrong with the other. A burst of thunder sounded, causing the windows to rattle. *This storm is vicious tonight*, Mike thought. He walked back to the window, awed by nature's display of power.

"I'm getting there." Clearing his throat, Mike parted the blinds, peering into the night. "Look, Bryan, I'm serious. Stop worrying about me and focus on your family."

"That's exactly what I'm doing. You're my family too. I know what storms do to you, man." Bryan voiced his concern.

"Used to, used to do to me," whispered Mike. "I'm getting better every day."

Those words had been Mike's mantra for the last three months. Starting out, they were just words of hope. Now they were words of truth, he was healing every day.

He could feel the memories of that horrible day trying to resurface. It had been three years since that day of hell. That was what he had personally named it. The worst of the scars were hidden from the world to see. The emotional and spiritual scars, those took time to heal. He learned it was a process that could not be rushed. His brother's voice pulled him from the ghosts of the past.

"Will you be able to make it Sunday?" Bryan asked hopefully.

Mike heard the caution in his brother's voice and knew there was ground for it. His self-imposed isolation caused a caution block between him and his family and friends. But they easily forgave him. He knew that he had hurt his brother the most. It was the first time in his life he had turned away from his beloved twin. Pain can make a person do things they normally would not do.

Mike had been a mess at the time. Hurt and guilt was his constant companions. Somehow the accident made him feel less of a man. Growing up, it was instilled in Mike that a man's duty was to love and protect his family. He had failed miserably on both accounts. Shaking his head, he refused to fall into the pit of pity. It was time to live again.

"I will be there," Mike said.

"Good, because Mama's been raving about a new healthy, but delicious recipe she's preparing for Pop. Plus, she's making both our favorite dishes. Sunday, we will be fed spiritually and physically," Bryan said.

"I'm salivating already. I can't wait."

"You're a wise man."

"But there is one who is wiser."

"His name is Jesus," they ended in unison.

Smiling, Mike replaced the phone in its cradle. Their father always said that to them in parting. Now they adopted the saying for themselves, hoping one day to pass it along to their sons. Bryan was ahead of him in the family department. Mike did not know if he would ever be ready again.

"Okay, Jesus, I'm relying on You as I start this new journey. Give me the strength to do what is needed of me," Mike said aloud to himself.

He was feeling a little out of sorts. He could hear the rain pelting against the window. The drops reminded him of teardrops. He never allowed himself that one good, ugly cry, the one where you lose control of your facial fluids and don't care. He recalled his father preaching a sermon titled *Releasing Your Tears to Heal*.

His father's words were still in his ear. They were so tangible; he looked around the room to see if his father was actually in the room. Mike closed his eyes and listened. *"There will come a time in a person's life, where they have to get ugly with God.*

No, I'm not talking attitude ugly, I'm talking about revealing the ugliness in you. The pain of rejection and hurt are ugly entities. They can cause you to do the things you normally would not do."

Mike was in a battle against himself. How could he accept the call to forgive? He had failed his family. Was it his time to be healed? He shook his head, suddenly overwhelmed with the need to get low. He fell to his knees, head bowed, and his breath coming in small sobs, beginning to escalate.

He continued to listen to his father's words in his ear. "*Sometimes we are embarrassed to show our ugliness to each other. Therefore, we become reserved, monitoring how much we reveal. However, the ugly cry with God, there is no monitoring. Truth be told, there really is no time for thought formulation. Your mind is on remote, your heart becomes the speaker, a sincere heart that is. Get ugly beloved. Allow your healing to come forth. Let it seep into every core of your being. Deep into your soul; refreshing is coming. The breath of life is breathing into you right now. Do not shut the door to His divine healing. Hurt and rejection will make you hesitant and not believe. If there be no believing, there can be no healing.*"

Mike remembered his father's soulful eyes moving over the congregation. Extending his hands toward the congregation, he would smile. "*I speak to your hearts this morning. You are in need of refreshments. You are thirsty for healing and renewal. You're dried out from the burden you have been carrying. Drink from the fountain of healing. Release yourselves, beloved.*"

Raw emotions were siphoning through him. The prominent one being guilt, its tentacles' refusing to release him. *You failed. What kind of man can't protect his own family? You survived, why?* Mike squeezed his eyes tight, trying desperately to block out the chaos in his head.

His father's wizened voice had become his life coach. He was helping him to live all over again. He needed to get a little lower. Mike stretched out on his stomach. He was filled with words to say, but didn't know how to say them. He was angry at not being able to protect his family, angry that he had survived. And yes, he was angry with God. He was always afraid to admit that.

If he told his family he was angry with God, they would probably send him off to some mental institution, never to speak to him again. No one should dare question or get angry with God, right? Well, he was filled to capacity with questions.

Mike's eyes flew open. "Why God? I don't understand. We were going to start our family together. Where were you? Why did You allow this to happen? I'm at a loss here." He pounded the floor in frustration. "I'm hurting. Maybe it's my punishment for failing her, for failing You." Mike didn't think he deserved to be forgiven. Not just yet. It couldn't be that easy. Why was he still alive and not his wife?

"Take no thought! I sense the battle of mind and spirit. It is time; you've been carrying this too long. Do not grieve the Holy Spirit. Accept His invitation and be healed. I cannot linger on this clarion call for long. You have to decide, beloved. Healing or hurt; deliverance or captivity. It's your choice. Release it completely now." Mike father's voice sounded again in his mind.

Mike had always been afraid that if he released it, he would lose himself completely. But tonight was different, he felt it was time to let go. It was time to heal. He stopped struggling. From his low position, he saw his dirty boots under his bed. He hadn't realized how dirty they were.

He ignored the howling of the wind. He ignored the falling rain. He ignored guilt's claim. Inhaling deeply, he expelled a shaky breath. Then the memories came in fragments. His wife was smiling trustingly at him. The image made Mike cry out loud. Shaking his head, he tried to rise, but couldn't. The memories continued.

His wife placed his hand on her stomach. *"I'm only three months, sweetie. I'm hardly showing,"* she said.

Mike began to perspire, his breath escalating. He was nervous about becoming a father. *"I will be happy with whatever God blesses us with, but I hope it's a boy that looks just like you."* His wife cupped his cheek.

The memories still hurt. Mike reared his head back, roaring

14

out his frustrations. He sounded like a wounded animal; the sound was frightening even to him. He began purging himself from the guilt. He had done all he could to protect his family that night. He began to crawl towards his nightstand. Reaching for his Bible, he clutched it tightly, as if it were a lifeline. He couldn't stop trembling.

"I need help. Help me, Father. Forgive me, Jesus. It is too much for me. I need to be free from my gilded cage of guilt." Falling to the floor, he allowed his tears to flow freely. Again, the images came fast and furious, causing him to cry out, remembering that night all too well.

* * *

Mike remembered that fateful night. They had just eaten at their favorite restaurant and were on their way home to pack their clothing. They had agreed to leave town that night. It was his wife's idea. She wanted a new beginning for them and their child. Mike knew that if she had asked for the sun, he would have given it to her. He was not concerned about his job, as he owned his own online legal management consultation services to legal organizations. He euphorically decided to focus on the now. He would work at the particulars when they settled into their new home.

The storm came out of nowhere. His wife seemed a little antsy that night. Mike contributed her emotional state to the pregnancy; juxtaposed with the sudden storm. His wife placed his hand on her slightly rounded stomach. He recalled their back tire blowing, and getting out to fix it; when the sudden bright lights from a car blinded him. The car remained idle. No one got out. The car engine revved up, the sound was taunting.

Mike squinted against the blinding car light, trying to see. The hairs on the back of his neck stood at attention, something was not right. He backpedaled slowly, glancing into their car. He met his wife's eyes. They were wide with fear. He smiled comfortingly at her. He saw something flash in her eyes, but couldn't place the emotion. Her lips trembled and she shook her head, mouthing the words *I love you*. The strange car revved up again, and every nerve ending in Mike screamed danger.

The car began to creep forward slowly before ramming into their vehicle. Mike felt himself being catapulted into the air. He landed roughly in a ditch. He heard a loud crashing sound, and his wife frantically screaming for help. Mike tried like hell to stay awake, to help his wife, but his body refused to cooperate. The last thing he remembered thinking was that he had failed his family.

* * *

Mike slowly opened his eyes, disoriented, he looked around. Awareness slowly set in, he was in his bedroom. He must have passed out. He lied there, breathing in and out, allowing the moment to register with him. Finally, he crawled to his bed, reaching for his dirty boots. He rose and went into the bathroom. He allowed the water to wash away the dirt from his boots. Rinsing his mouth out, he looked at his image in the mirror.

He had remembered everything. It was not his fault; he was finally able to accept what everyone tried to tell him. He felt different. Lighter somehow. Mike walked toward his bedroom, placing his now clean boots by the door. He would wear them tomorrow.

Going to the window, he looked out into the night. At last it had stopped raining. The sun was slowly making its ascent. That was how Mike was feeling. He was finally seeing the light at the end of the tunnel.

He remembered a passage in the Bible, when Jesus spoke a word to the winds and waves, causing them to calm. "You really are a storm stopper." Mike smiled confidently. "I have a feeling everything is going to be all right." He returned to his bed. For the first time in many years, he slept peacefully.

Chapter 2

The irritating sound of the phone was persistent. She refused to answer the call, but it was a useless battle. Rolling over, she reluctantly answered the phone.

"Hello."

"I've been calling you for thirty minutes now." The voice sounded agitated.

"Maybe it was a sign that I was sleeping." Glancing at her alarm clock, Sheila frowned. "Like any normal person would be at 8 o'clock in the morning."

"I knew you'd forget or try to come up with an excuse not to come today," Rayna said.

"What are you talking about? Look, Rayna, call me back in two years, would ya?" Sheila groused.

"Don't you dare hang up that phone, Sheila! You're accompanying me to church today, and that's final. You promised me." Sheila could hear a car honking in the background. "Please, Mother Hattie, get off the road. There should be a law on senior citizens driving."

"Rayna, isn't she one of the Mothers at your church? I don't think she'd take kindly to your wanting to band her from driving herself to church." Sheila could not resist taunting her best friend.

"Whatever. Stop trying to distract me from my cause of the day." Sheila smiled at being considered a cause.

Rayna was a true activist. She often expressed how important it is to live a proactive lifestyle instead of a reactive one. And to not wait until tragedy occurs to tell your loved ones you love them. If someone was hurting, she wanted to heal them. If anyone was lost, she wanted to find them.

"I'll be at your house in twenty minutes. Twenty minutes, Sheila. There is no negotiation on this!" The dial tone enforced the command.

Sheila fell back against the soft mounds of pillows, burying herself deeper under the covers. "Me and my big mouth. Maybe she will go away if I don't let her in." She yawned, hoping to get a little more sleep. Groaning, Sheila shot straight up. "I forgot I gave her a key. Me and my big mouth," she reiterated.

Glancing at the clock, it revealed she had fifteen minutes to get dressed. Sheila pushed the cover off of her, and began kicking and screaming. She was suddenly ashamed of such childlike behavior, but couldn't help admitting to herself it felt good. She remembered watching one of those self-help programs, which indicated that one should never hold in their frustrations. Finding a healthy way to release it was one of the keys to a healthy lifestyle.

Making her way to the shower, she laughed. Rayna was her best friend, but they were polar opposites. Rayna was vibrant and outspoken, where she was more reserved with her feelings. They met at Stanford University in the Registrar's office; the line was ridiculously long.

In Rayna's fashion, she stuck her hand out and introduced herself. Sheila had noticed her the moment she entered. Who would not, she was stunningly beautiful; tall with creamy brown skin. Her hair gave testament of her mixed lineage. The long dark tresses hung down her back. Her eyes were a light caramel color, and always reminded Sheila of the sun.

"Hi, I'm Rayna Peterson, I'm from Detroit."

"Hi, I'm Sheila Lawson from North Carolina."

"Tar heel." Rayna smiled, referring to the State's moniker.

"All the way baby," Sheila replied proudly.

The two have been inseparable since. Rayna majored in Pre-law/Political Science. Sheila majored in Sociology. Both women were studious by choice. Sacrificing leisure activities, they both maintained exceptional good grades. Together they made the decision to move to Atlanta, Georgia.

Rayna now works for the law firm Hudson, Fist and Hudson. In a couple of years, she wanted to make partner. Sheila strongly believed she would too. When Rayna wanted something bad, she usually got it. Her tenacity was awe-inspiring, and at times scary.

Sheila worked at The Mending Heart. It was a facility for abused and exploited women. The money left something to be desired. However, that was not what her heart was after. She felt she was called to the center to help those women.

The doorbell chimed out the song *Ave Marie*, Sheila's favorite song of all times. Rayna loved the song *Ave Marie* as well; but bulked when Sheila announced her idea to install it as a doorbell ring tone. Becoming acclimated to it, Rayna too had a ring tone installed in her condominium. True to her character, her doorbell's ring tone selection was *An Everlasting Love* by Natalie Cole. Sheila could not help but to wonder if there was a sublime meaning behind Rayna's selection.

"I'm letting myself in since you've got the pace of Mother Hattie this morning. And if you tell her I said that, I'll plead the Fifth and never speak to you again." Rayna said all of this in a single breath. Her footsteps faded into the kitchen. Sheila mentally counted to three. "Girl, when are you going to start eating and save this, if you can call it food, for the rabbits? Rayna frowned at the fresh raw vegetables and skim milk in Sheila's refrigerator. Sheila was extremely health conscious. "Sweetie, some men love a little meat on their women," Rayna said laughing.

Sheila mumbled and glanced down at her curvy figure. She paused in putting on her earrings. "I like my rabbit food, it gives me energy and it's healthy," she called out.

Rayna retrieved a cartoon of milk from the refrigerator. "Yeah, yeah, whatever," she groused.

Opening one of the kitchen cupboards, Rayna retrieved a medium sized bowl. Fixing herself a liberal amount of Raisin Bran, and pouring a healthy dose of 2% milk on the cereal, she seated herself at the island table and began to eat, waiting for Sheila.

After about five minutes, Sheila walked in smiling.

"Good morning, and don't you look enchanting," Rayna said.

Sheila turned in a circular motion, showing off her outfit. "Thank you, sweetie. You're rubbing off on me, sister girl."

"Well, I'm just doing my duty as your true best friend and fashion advisor." Sheila sent an air kiss in Ryana's direction. "I'm excited about service today." Rayna suddenly clapping her hands together made Sheila jump. "I'm excited because Pastor Montgomery's son is preaching today. Last week, he was installed as the Assistant Pastor of Deliverance Missionary Hope Church."

Sheila couldn't refrain from rolling her eyes. "I know, because you've only told me that three hundred times." She snagged two bottles of tomato juice from the refrigerator, offering one to Rayna. Grimacing, Rayna opted for bottled water. Sheila gave her a bottled water, and then seated herself next to her best friend.

"This is good news. Pastor Montgomery has been the Pastor for over thirty years, and he needed help. In the Bible Moses' Uncle Jethro told him he needed help, because the burden of the people was too much for him to carry alone." Rayna took a huge gulp from the bottled water, becoming quiet.

"That's a good thing, right?" Sheila queried.

Replacing the top on the bottled water, Rayna smiled. "It is a wonderful thing. I was just thinking about Bryan and Michael." Sheila's brows furrowed in confusion. "They're Pastor Montgomery's identical twin sons. Bryan is now the Assistant Pastor, and is married to a wonderful woman, Valerie. They have two-month old twins, a girl and a boy." Rayna's voice trailed off.

Instinctively, Sheila embraced Rayna. "It's okay to mourn over a loss, Rayna. You don't have to play the superwoman role with me. I'm your best friend. Keep it real with me," she said.

Rayna allowed the embrace to last longer than she normally would have. She did not do pity. "I'm alright, and I'm not playing a role. I know who I am. This is my burden to carry. I don't understand the why of it. However, I will weather it." She glanced at her delicate gold wristwatch. "Let's go before we're late."

* * *

The church edifice was beatific to look upon. It was nestled in downtown Atlanta. It was set a ways off from the highway, giving it a suburban feel. The landscape was utterly gorgeous. Five large maple trees stood erect. Flowers of all kind were in full bloom, their sweet scents wafting in the wind.

Sheila wanted to stop and literally smell the roses. She never recalled a church having rose bushes. Rayna informed Sheila earlier that the church had undergone some great changes since being built forty-five years ago. The changes were necessary, because yearly their membership showed no signs of slowing down.

Deliverance Missionary Hope Church now held 1200 members strong. Rayna was an active member of the church; serving as legal advisor, and was a member of the Women's Board and Missionary Board. Sheila was the opposite. She was quite uncomfortable with church. This was her first time in years attending service.

"Relax. Pastor Montgomery is not one of those fire and brimstone types of preachers. He tells it like it is, yet in a unique ministering way. I'm sure his son, Bryan, inherited some of his chutzpa for the preaching of the Word."

Sheila eyes were soft with concern. "Is it always this packed in here?" she asked, as they walked into the church.

Hearing the nervousness in Sheila's voice, Rayna squeezed her hand in support. "Word must have gotten out that Bryan would be preaching today. Thank God I asked Sister Huxtable to reserve our seats."

An usher embraced both women then led them into the sanctuary. Sheila felt sweat coursing down her back. It seemed as if they were being led to the front of the church. She wanted to stop Rayna and run out of the church. Everyone appeared to be looking at her. The usher led them to the third row. They were so close to the pulpit; Sheila could see the members of the choir warming up for their musical selections. The atmosphere was charged with excitement. Looking around, she couldn't find one sad face in the congregation.

LOVE FOUND ME

"It's like this every Sunday. Only it's more intense today," Rayna said. A tall elegantly clad man approached the pulpit, Rayna nudged Sheila. "That's Deacon Frye. He's a powerhouse too. And can sing like no other."

"Praise the Lord. It is good to be here. Look at your neighbor in greeting and declare that this morning," Deacon Frye said.

The congregation repeated the greeting. The words sounded like swarming bees to Sheila's ears. Strangely enough, she felt comforted by the sound and smiling faces.

"After Sister Bethany has blessed us with the selection of *Falling in Love with Jesus,* Pastor Bryan Montgomery will break the bread of Heaven with us," Deacon Frye announced.

A beautiful woman took the place Deacon Frye vacated. She reminded Sheila of a contestant from *American Idol,* who went on to do movies, winning her an Oscar in the process.

Smiling, she opened her mouth, and the sound coming forth was simply enchanting. Some people were blessed with the talent to sing, while others were blessed with a gift to sing. This young woman was gifted. That was the right song to sing that day. The words were penetrating. Sheila felt herself being pricked by them.

Falling in love with Jesus
Falling in love with Jesus
Falling in love with Jesus
was the best thing I ever, ever done
In His arms, I feel protected
In His arms never disconnected
In His arms I feel protected
there's no place I'd rather be

"Excuse me, Sister." Sheila looked up at the same usher that had seated them smiling face. "Would you be kind enough to move down one so Brother Montgomery can be seated?" Rayna and Sheila scooted one seat down.

Sheila immediately became aware of Brother Montgomery's cologne. It was exotic, but she couldn't place its name.

"Thank you," he said.

His voice sent shock waves coursing through her. It reminded her of the quiet after the storm. Looking up, Sheila literally lost her breath. His eyes, they were mesmerizing, but that was not what she was looking at. She was looking past the beauty of his eyes, past his breathtaking smile. She actually wanted to put her arms around him in comfort, and a perfect stranger no less! She looked into his eyes, and was again jolted by their effect. She felt as though she knew him somehow. That was impossible; she could never forget one such as him.

"You're welcome," Sheila said, forcing herself not to fidget under his perusal. He was one breathtaking man dressed in a dark blue three-piece suit. His skin was the color of dark chocolate, and he sported a goatee, which gave him a dashing look.

Sheila felt the song, *Falling In Love With Jesus,* words were having a different affect because of the stranger's presence. It made her think of love. She did not think true love exited, as she never had a model to follow. Growing up in a foster care had a way of shaping how a person viewed couples relationships. Sheila, years ago, became resolved to the fact that love was not for her. She didn't have anything in her to give, and was certain no one wanted to give love to her. Maybe she was unlovable. Truth be told; she wasn't sure she knew how to love a husband. Were there any written rules on how to do so? In any case, she was happy working at the center, and if she never got married, it would be all right with her.

"Thank you, Sister Bethany." Deacon Frye's cheerful voice pulled Sheila from her silent introspection. "Let us welcome Pastor Bryan Montgomery." The young man stepping forth caused Sheila to glance sharply at her neighbor. It was like looking into a mirror.

The stranger smiled at her reaction. "We get that a lot. Hi, I'm Mike." He offered his hand.

Sheila could not believe she was actually sitting next to the pastor's son. This was far above her comfort level. She definitely wanted to exit stage left immediately. Clearing her throat, she hesitantly clasped Mike's extended hand. Her eyes widened at the jolt running up her arm. She looked sharply at Mike, and knew that he too felt it.

"It's nice to meet you. I'm Sheila." She felt as if she were on television, because it seemed as if the whole congregation was looking at her. The hushed murmurs did not escape her attention. Neither could she ignore the many looks of disdain that several single women were sending her way. They too recognized that she was sitting in the wrong seat. Maybe it was her nerves. The illusion seemed all too real. Literally, their attitudes confirmed Sheila's self-talk that it was a bad idea attending service today. She vowed she would never return.

Rayna nudged Sheila in friendly rebuke. "I'm Rayna, Sheila's best friend," she whispered, offering her hand to Mike.

"Pleasure to meet you, Rayna," he whispered back.

"I'm happy to be here amongst you, my family," Pastor Byran's voice interrupted. *His voice is a replica of his brother's*, Sheila thought. Only his did not send electrical currents racing through her.

"When the Lord spoke to me to move back home; I had no idea that His plans included my becoming Assistant Pastor." Bryan's eye rested on his father, who smiled. "*For My thoughts are not your thoughts, neither are your ways My ways, says the Lord.* I want to preach briefly from the book of Matthew 11:28-30." As was his father's habit, young Pastor Montgomery eyes scanned the congregation. His eyes rested on his wife and children. They were sitting in the front row. His wife, whom many people likened her to Michelle Obama, was dressed in a soft lavender two-piece suit. Her Bible already opened, rested gently on her lap. She smiled and nodded.

Returning the nod, Pastor Bryan proceeded to read the Bible's passage. "*Come to me, all you who labor and are heavy laden, and I will give you rest. Take my yoke upon you and learn from me, for I am gentle and lowly in heart, and you will find rest for your souls. For my yoke is easy and my burden is light."*

Sheila felt her heart constrict as Pastor Bryan read the Bible passages. His voice was soothingly melodic. It made listeners want to sit down at his feet as he expounded the written Word. She sat up straighter, listening with her heart.

"Today, beloved, I want to speak to your heart. I pray that you allow me to do so. Allow me access to your spirit. I want to get past the many layers of hurt so you can hear me. Past the rejections so you can receive me. What you're carrying is too heavy for you," Pastor Bryan stated.

Sheila felt a stirring within. It felt as though he was talking directly to her. She was tired of being a carrier of rejection. She wanted desperately to be free, but how? She had been carrying this burden for so long, she did not know where to begin for the healing to take place. She saw something white out of her peripheral vision.

Turning, she saw Mike offering her his handkerchief. Sheila touched her cheeks. She was shocked to find them wet. Nodding her head, she accepted his offering. Straightening her shoulders and lifting her chin, she vowed she would not feel embarrassed. This was her moment of renewal, and she would embrace it.

Mike's eyes moved over Sheila's face. He could see the inward battle she was facing. Her face was just that transparent. He wanted desperately to take away her pain. Mike shook his head at that revelation. This woman was a stranger. Yet, he felt like he knew her somehow. Something about her was calling to him, and he wanted to answer the call.

Hazarding another look at Sheila, he was struck by how beautiful she was. Her skin was clear and healthy. Her hair was full and shiny, softly resting against slender shoulders. Yet, he sensed a hurt within her. Mike wanted to know what caused her hurt. He wanted to know the core of her. What was her love level for God? That was of extreme importance to him.

LOVE FOUND ME

Realizing it was going to take patience and prayer on his part, he smiled. Mike quickly offered up a prayer for guidance to win the heart of Sheila. That acknowledgement caused Mike to briefly stop breathing. Where did that come from? Why would he want to win the heart of a stranger? It was strange, but he could have declared he'd met Sheila somewhere before. It felt as though he knew her. Expelling a shaky breath, Mike felt the need, and it was a need to pursue this lady next to him, and that he would.

He knew the exact moment Sheila won the battle over her inward war. He was proud of her, and wanted to tell her so, but felt that would only make Sheila feel ill at ease. Therefore, he did what he wanted to do most. Very gently, he reached out and held her hand and she let him.

"That is why God says to come," Pastor Bryan said. He didn't raise his voice, it remained the same. It was so compelling. "It's your decision to release the hurt. I sense that many of you are hurting. Your hurt may have come from a friend, your parents, or husband or wife. Whatever it is, you must let it go. And it is your choice to do so. I know this may be much more difficult for some than others." Pastor Bryan paused, allowing his gaze to roam over the congregation. Sheila stilled when his gaze met and held hers. "Difficult, yes beloved, but not impossible."

Several people began making their way to the altar. The same soloist took the microphone and began to sing *Caught Up To See Jesus* by Kirk Franklin. A young woman, dressed in a pair of tattered old jeans and a wrinkled T-shirt, hastily made her way down to the altar. She looked neither left nor right. Sheila was inspired by her boldness, but couldn't move.

"The Bible says to come as you are. Many think God is referring to clothing, but He's referring to broken, whole, sad, happy, lost and found. Come, He is no respecter of persons. He wants you. He cares for you."

Pastor Bryan stopped in front of the woman with the torn jeans. He bent down and whispered something in her ear. The woman began to sob loudly; falling to her knees, crying out, "Thank You, Lord, for forgiving me. Thank You, Lord, for forgiving me!"

Pastor Bryan's sermon on forgiveness and love touched the heart of many that day. Sheila looked around, and noticed she was not the only one moved to tears. At the end of Pastor Bryan's sermon, several attendees assembled at the altar when the call to receive salvation was offered. Sheila was glad she stayed. The end result was worth it.

Chapter 3

Bryan was closing his briefcase when the door to his study opened.

"Wonderful sermon, Pastor Montgomery," Mike said, smiling at his replica. Coming from behind his desk, Bryan returned his twin's smile.

"You came. Good to see you, man." The brothers embraced each other. Pulling away, Bryan wiped his eyes.

The brothers' love for each other ran deeply. It was true when they said twins shared a sixth sense. They would normally know what the other would be thinking. They found themselves finishing each other's sentences. When one of them was down, they could usually sense it. It was just uncanny. Yet, they were comfortable with their unique bond.

"Hey, this is a day of celebration, so no heavy stuff today," Mike affectionately admonished.

"Indeed. When you said you were coming, I had my reservations." Bryan rounded his desk, reaching for his coat and briefcase.

Putting his hands in his pockets, Mike bowed his head. "I don't fault you. I've let you guys down so many times before." He captured his brother's eyes again. "It's true what I told you on the phone. I'm getting better every day." Mike and Bryan both exited his study.

"Good. Because I miss creaming my baby brother in B-ball on Saturdays, and now that you're back, let's get it started again." Bryan was referring to their once a week basketball games. Their meetings served both as a tension releaser and catch up time between the two brothers. Their games could oftentimes become intense, depending on the situation in their lives. Judging by the tension emanating from his twin, Bryan was pretty sure their game was going to be hot as the Sahara desert.

Once Mike and Bryan got outside, Mike paused when he

saw her. She was chatting with Mother Hattie and another woman.

"Bryan, who is that?" Mike inquired.

He had already acquired her name during service; he was hoping Bryan would supply him with a little more information on her. Mike felt a little guilty asking for information behind her back. He wanted to approach her and ask her to have dinner with him, but instinct told him she would only decline his invitation. The last thing he wanted was for her to run from him.

Bryan looked toward the direction Mike indicated. "Who, Mother Hattie?" he asked.

"No. The woman in the blue dress," Mike replied distractedly.

"Oh, that's Sheila Lawson. I only know her by name, because her friend is Sister Rayna Peterson, who talks often of her." Bryan looked sharply at Mike. It was the first time in years he had expressed an interest in any woman.

Mike already knew her name, he was thirsting for more. Was she dating? Was she married? What was her favorite color? He stood there watching her, while Bryan watched him. Mike didn't say anything; he didn't have to, as his eyes said it all. He was struck by Sheila's beauty.

Her head was slightly tilted, and the sun was causing the reddish tint to come alive in her shoulder length tresses. Mike felt like she captured the sun. He suddenly felt illuminated and giddy looking at her. He stilled the fact that what he was feeling was a shock to him. He hadn't felt anything for a woman since his wife died. He looked at the woman again. She smiled. Mike swallowed hard, suddenly assaulted with the need to hear her voice, to discover her likes and dislikes.

She was petite and was casually dressed. Somehow, Mike knew that underneath her exterior, was a woman filled with a passion to succeed at anything she went after. He found himself wanting to be a part of that equation. She laughed at something Mother Hattie said. Mike felt as though someone solar plexed him, the sound was melodic. He couldn't shake the feeling that she was familiar to him somehow, yet he knew he had never met her before.

Nodding at Mother Hattie, Sheila and Rayna shared a laugh with her before walking away. Mike watched them as they entered a Silver BMW. He watched them as their car pulled out of the parking lot until it faded from sight. Bryan watched Mike and smiled. His brother was smitten, that was obvious to see, as his beloved twin could not take his eyes off of Sheila. Bryan felt hope surfacing, and immediately clung to it, but he couldn't help but to wonder, why Sheila?

Sure, to the natural eye she was beautiful. But what was she like on the inside, is what mattered most. Bryan wanted his brother to love again. He deserved the best, and he had suffered enough. Bryan noticed his brother was still staring in the direction the car had taken. He clasped his brother on the back and smiled. He had a feeling everything was going to be alright.

No one saw the dark figure watching them from across the street. Looking at the worn photo, there was no doubt she was the one. It was all falling into place. "Soon, real soon," the figure said, before turning and walking away.

* * *

Sheila couldn't shake the feeling that she was being watched. She looked once more out of her side view mirror.

"What's wrong with you? You're acting like *I Spy*, and don't try to deny it. That makes the seventh time you've looked in that mirror in the last ten minutes," Rayna said.

Sheila sighed. "I don't know. For the past couple of days, I've been feeling like someone is watching me." She laughed nervously.

Everything inside Rayna stilled. She briefly glanced at Sheila before returning her eyes to the road. Sheila's eyes roamed over Rayna's face, and immediately knew she was remembering a time long ago.

"Really? Sheila, if you've got this feeling then you should

take it seriously. You remember our instructor teaching us how we should rely on our instincts for survival. If your radars are going off, listen to them." Rayna voice trembled slightly.

Sheila could have kicked herself for opening up that can of worms.

"Look, Rayna, I'm sure it's just my nerves getting the best of me. My work sometimes tends to follow me home. Policy is, we are not to get close to the women at the shelter, but how can I not. I feel for them."

Quiet settled in the car. Both women's mind went back to the past.

"Sheila, just be true to your personality. I don't know what I would have done without you in my life. The world would be a better place if we had more of you in it," Rayna said sincerely.

"Look, let's go to Bernie's. I want something greasy and fattening." Sheila laughed out loud at the look Rayna was sending her.

Rayna's mouth opened in mock shock. "No way, not little Ms. Health conscious."

"I know it's crazy, but after that sermon, I'm feeling charged and free. I feel adventurous, feel like doing something different. I can let loose sometimes, right?"

"Amen, sister girl. That's what I've been trying to tell your stuck up self for awhile now."

Sheila held up one hand. "I know you just didn't insult me like that. Me, your BFF?"

Rayna stuck her tongue out at Sheila. "Yes, you are my best friend for life, so take it in love, honey. But look, if I'm going to get a burger, it's going to be a good burger. Let's go to the Caddy Shack. Their burgers are the best in the world. I even emailed Gayle King, hoping she'd feature it on Oprah."

"Are you serious?"

"I'm serious as a lark in water."

Sheila believed her. "Well, let's do the thing then."

Amazingly, both their stomachs growled at the same time.

They both laughed. Rayna leaned over and turned on the radio, filling the car with the sound of gospel recording artist Tye Tribbett's, *I Want It All Back*. Both women began to sing the lyrics loud and proud. They both possessed wonderful voices, but chose to sing in an off key and free manner. Sheila was glad for the reprieve, but still was unable to shake off the feeling of being watched.

Chapter 4

Mike was immediately flooded with childhood memories. He was parked in front of his parents' home. The two-story house had undergone a major overhaul. He barely recognized the place. His mother was known for her garden. Every year, she participated in the Azalea Fest, and every year, without fail, she would win some type of award for her hard work.

Bryan knocked softly on his car window. "Ready?" Mike nodded his head and exited his vehicle. Just then, a medium-sized woman opened the front door. She was wearing a frilly apron that read *Number 1 Chef*.

She had smooth pecan skin, and her salt and peppered hair was stylishly cut. She stood in the doorway in greeting, smiling broadly as her boys approached her. She was always amazed at how much they looked like their father.

"Hey, babies, you two come right on in and get washed up now. Dinner is in ten minutes." Turning slightly, she paused, giving them the look. "Not a second earlier or later," she said.

Growing up, the twins knew when they had incurred their mother's wrath. *The look* said it all. That look was all it took to discipline them growing up. Even now, as grown men, they still obeyed "*the look*." Bryan bent down and kissed his mother on the cheek, and Mike mirrored his brother's action.

Mrs. Montgomery held the embrace slightly long. She loved both her boys. Although her boys were identical, they deferred in their personalities. She had noticed this from their infant development. Bryan cried the most, alerting her to his discomforts. Mike was more subdued, he hardly ever cried. She had to decipher his needs and wants. It is still the same to this day. Mike's loss caused him to retreat, shutting himself off from friends and loved ones. He would never know the magnitude of how much his actions had hurt her.

She hardly slept; she walked the floor day and night. This

would go on for several months. The stress was finally taking its toll on her body. She was losing weight, and her blood pressure had elevated. Again, she had to make one of the most difficult decisions in her life. She let Mike go. She placed him in God's hands, and again, God has not let her down. She was reminded of the prodigal son in the Bible. Her son had finally come home. She smiled, offering up a small prayer of thanks. Mike stepped back and winked at his mother.

"Clara, will you let my boys in. Even in their older days you're still spoiling them," their father said.

"Herb that is what mothers are supposed to do to her boys. And since God saw fit to bless me with two wonderful now grown men, I'm doubling up on the loving." This time Mama winked. Turning, she went into the house, with Mike and Bryan imitating her hurried steps.

After freshening up, Mama led them into a palatial dining room. The aroma had Mike salivating. He smiled over roasted turkey, candied yams, macaroni and cheese, and other tasty looking health items for his father. He knew that dessert was going to be off the chain. He believed his mama's second calling was to be a chef. She was fierce when it came to her family well beings.

As the matriarch of the family, Clara Montgomery did not play. Family was first and foremost. Mike and Bryan looked at each other and smiled. Mama and Papa caught their action, and immediately exchanged one of their own. It felt like old times. Ordinarily, Bryan's wife and kids would have joined them, but she had made plans earlier to have dinner with her own parents. After saying grace, they commenced with dinner.

"Son that was a mighty fine sermon you preached today. I couldn't have preached it any better." Pop smiled over a spoonful of macaroni and cheese. He was stunned by how good it actually tasted. It was one of his wife's healthy recipes.

Mr. Montgomery was a handsome man; his head was sprinkled lightly with gray hair. The twins were a younger version of him; they inherited their father's height. All three men were six feet two with broad shoulders.

"Thanks Pop. I had no idea that I was going to be preaching that particular message. I opened my mouth to speak the message I studied, and was suddenly compelled to go in another direction." Bryan's voice sounded awed.

"Son, we are just instruments used to get His message across. He is the orchestra, we just follow His movements. My sermons have been changed on many occasions. He interrupted our regularly scheduled program to meet the needs of His people."

Mike was always humbled by the discussions between his brother and Father. He couldn't recall a day in his life he ever felt envious of his twin. But what he was experiencing now came close to it he supposed. He swallowed hard. He had difficulties hearing God. What kept him grounded was his family upbringing. Their family source was faith in God and each other. Totally seeing the faith his parents, and now brother, displayed was humbling. Mike wanted to chime in with his brother and Father about how he too could hear God speaking to him, but couldn't. He just couldn't hear God. Truth be told, sometimes he felt like God didn't like him, and that He tolerated him for the sake of his family. Mike sighed at that thought. Looking up, he was startled to see three sets of eyes on him.

Mike frowned. "Did I miss something?" he asked.

Mama smiled softly, taking a dainty bite from her baked chicken. "I said have you met anyone in particular yet?" Mike realized he had drifted off from their conversation of Bryan's sermon, and that they had now moved on to his non-existent love life.

Mike's stomach dropped at the question. He braced himself for what was coming next. He glanced at his father and brother. Bryan nodded in sympathy. Pop was focused on his meal.

Mrs. Montgomery waved her fork animatedly in the air, her eyes wide with excitement. "Because my friend, Jessica, you remember her, don't you, sweetie? We attended college together; she's my Zeta Phi Beta sister." She gushed with pride at the mentioning of her sorority name. "Well, her daughter, Lillian, has just returned home from graduating from Law School. She is a lovely woman; I have met her three times already and..."

"Now Clara..." Pop cautioned, never once glancing up from his meal.

Mama looked at Pop with a wounded expression on her face. Mike wasn't fooled, neither was Bryan, who hid a smile. Their mother was tough as nails. She was also wise, never once had she ever disrespected her husband. Having both grown up in a single parent household; they vowed to never go to bed angry with each other. Forty-five years later, they have still held true to their vow. If they were in a disagreement, they found a way to work it out, or they'd peacefully agreed to disagree.

Mrs. Montgomery waved her hand nonchalantly. "Well, I only asked because I was in my prayer closet concerning you. Once I was done, I took a brief nap. I dreamt you were standing at the altar, your bride was walking towards you, and all of a sudden, you ran," she said accusingly.

Bryan, who was sipping raspberry lemonade, began to cough and laugh hysterically. This garnered a scowl from Mike.

"Bryan, leave your brother alone. He probably had cold feet. It happens. I know I did the day I married your mother." Pop bit into a healthy sized turkey leg. "I didn't run though. Your mama would have tracked me down like a hunting dog tracks a deer."

"Herb, now you stop that, I would not have tracked you down. I'm too much of a lady for that." Mama sipped her juice. "I would have hired someone to do it for me."

"I heard that, Clara. You had my heart from the start. Unlike women, men take their time, but when we know she is the one, can't no one or nobody stop us from making our claim."

"I hear ya, Pop." Bryan raised his glass of lemonade to his father. "I knew I was ready. Man, I ran to and not away from my wife. When you know you found the right one, you pursue her. Ain't no need in playing around with it, good women are hard to find. So when God tells you she is the one, your gift, receive it."

"Now that sounds like something I taught you, son. Here, here." Pop raised his glass of lemonade in their traditional salute. Bryan lifted his in return, smiling like a Cheshire cat.

Mama shook her head. "We aren't possessions, you know. Women are true gifts from God, invaluable to men. I wish some women knew their true value, because they wouldn't allow themselves to settle for the first thing that comes along," Mama commented.

"When I saw your mama, I knew she was my gift from God." Pop winked at his wife, who blushed becomingly. "She spoke to my heart and soul." He held up one hand. "Not verbally. It was more of spirit to spirit dialogue."

Mrs. Montgomery tapped her glass with her fork. "Herb, sweetheart, you're not telling the whole story. If you're going to tell it, tell all of it."

Mike and Bryan smiled. They were familiar with how their parents met. They set back and waited for their father to begin.

"Clara, I said spiritually you spoke to me. I cannot help it if other women spoke naturally." Pop looked at Mike and Bryan. "Sons, your old man here was like a magnet. Everywhere I turned, the women were after me. They weren't really after me for myself. They wanted the title of being a first lady. It's distasteful at times. Men like a challenge. My case and point is I chose your mother, my little Angel of the field." Pop speared a baby carrot with his fork, popping it into his mouth.

Mama smiled, blushing again. "Uh huh. You're father was once bitten, twice shy. He had his guard up, and it took him awhile to lower it. Ninety percent of communication is nonverbal. Your father first spoke to me with his eyes, and then his heart." Her voice sounded far away.

Mr. Montgomery's dark eyes raked over his wife's face. They held each other's stare before he returned his attention to his meal.

Mrs. Montgomery shook her head. "His words were powerful, he was endowed with such revelation and knowledge at such a young age, and he was humble with it, too. I knew your father was the one when I first saw him though." She chuckled softly. "It sure wasn't his looks. And that wardrobe of his at the time, honey please! Corduroy pants should never have been invented."

The twins began to fidget; both were hard pressed to keep from laughing. Their father sent them a hard stare, immediately quelling their laughter.

"My heart, mind and soul were all in one accord. No doubts at all. It was a process, and great things can't be rushed. Some things were happenstance, and other things were planned. I happened to join the choir. Oops, he was already a member. I happened to be attending the church annual picnic. Oops, he was the director over the picnic. You get my meaning." Mama winked at her stunned twins.

Mike couldn't believe his mama had game. She was always so pristine and docile. This was the first time she told them her side of the story. Pop just continued to eat his food in his gustatory fashion.

"In the end, he noticed me, and eventually began to trust me both with his money and his heart." She stood up to refill her men's drinks. She caressed her husband's cheek in passing. Then she squeezed Bryan's hands after refilling his glass. When she got to Mike, she hugged him. "Baby, you can't always run from things." She glanced at her husband. "Sometimes you have to deal with an issue or lose yourself in the process. Besides, you aren't getting any younger; all your mojo is going to run dry soon. Utilize your youth while you can. Stop running." Mama refilled Mike's glass; returned to her seat and took a bite out of her chicken.

Pop looked mischievously at his wife and smiled. "Careful now, Clara, mind how you take a bite of things."

"Herb, now stop talking like that in front of the children." Mike and Bryan shared a smile at being called children. They'd long since conceded to the fact that their mother would forever see them as 'children'. She turned her attention to Mike. "Maybe you should talk to your father after dinner, baby." Mike looked at his mother confusingly. Mrs. Montgomery lowered her voice, raising one dark brow. "You know talk, talk. Then you will stop the running. A rolling stone gathers no moss."

Bryan was still coughing-laughing. Mike sat looking stunned. His parents were talking like the dream had actually taken place.

"Don't look like that, son. You know your mama's dreams have a tendency to come to pass," their father said.

Mike could not deny this, but it still didn't make it any easier to hear. The truth hurts. He had been running for years and had become good at it. He thought back to how he confessed his healing a couple of days ago. Yes, it was now time to stop running. He wanted to start his family. He looked at his parents and at his brother. Family was the center for them; it was solid as a rock. He couldn't help feeling something was missing. He remembered the Bible passage; *A man that finds a wife, finds a good thing.* Unexpectedly, his mind returned to the woman he saw in church today.

"Mom, I haven't officially met anyone yet, but when I do, you guys will be the first...uh, second to know," Mike said.

Wearing a small frown, Mama slowly lowered her fork. "Second? Sweetie there had better be a good explanation why your mother would be the second to know." Her voice was soft, but Mike was not fooled, she was seriously offended.

"God would be the first to know," Mike stated.

At that, his family burst into laughter. His father raised his glass, and the rest of them followed suit.

"Cheers to the future," Bryan declared.

"To family and faith," Mama praised.

"To good things coming," Pop proclaimed.

Mike looked at his father, who smiled mischievously. He couldn't help but to wonder if he knew something he didn't. *In time, God will reveal it in time, Mike thought.*

"To auspicious beginnings," Mike said, joining the toast.

Chapter 5

Turning her car's engine off, Rayna glanced up at the sky. It was a beautiful day. The sun was shining. The clouds decorated the sky with their soft billowy presence. When Rayna was a child, whenever she felt sad, scared and alone, and if the clouds were out like now, she would close her eyes and pretend she could fly up to the sky and sit on the clouds.

She learned in her psychology class that, that was a form of escapism. Although it may have worked for a child, it did not work that way for adults. In the real world, you have to deal with your problem. The issue was finding a way to deal with unexpected life changing issues. Rayna bowed her head, her thick tresses falling forward.

"Lord, I thank You for another day. I speak into existence that this will be a day of accomplishments. Pastor Montgomery's sermon yesterday was on love and forgiveness. I'm getting there. It's all I have now. However, I am trying."

Rayna screamed as something suddenly hit her car window. She glanced up into familiar eyes. Recognition quickly replaced shock. She rolled her window down. "Pastor Montgomery?"

Mike smiled, shaking his head. "Please don't insult me. I'm the better looking one."

Rayna's brows furrowed in confusion. *What was Mike doing at her place of business?*

Seeing her confusion, Mike explained. "I'm officially Attorney at Law for Hudson, Fist and Hudson."

Rayna's mouth dropped open in shock for the second time that morning. Shaking her head, she reached for her attaché case, and hurriedly exited her car. "You're the new guy?" she asked.

Her mouth did a repeat performance, which she immediately closed. She didn't want Mike to think she was some dim-witted woman, instead of the competent attorney that she was. She could not wait to call and tell Sheila this juicy tidbit of information. Her fingers were itching for her cellular. Mike smiled, bowing from the waist, old worldly style. *No he didn't*, she thought. Her fingers were really itching to call Sheila now, brother had excellent mannerism.

"I'm Michael Montgomery, lawyer extraordinaire at your service, mi lady," he said.

Laughing, Rayna curtsied in return "Your gallantness is duly noted and appreciated, kind sir. If you like, I could introduce you around the office."

"That won't be necessary. I met everyone last Friday. Well, I thought I had met everyone." He nodded his head at her. "Apparently I was wrong. It's only a matter of getting acclimated now."

"I was out of the office last Friday. Had to do some investigating for a case I'm working on."

Mike extended his left hand, indicating for Rayna to precede him. Nodding her head, she walked forward.

"Look, I didn't mean to startle you earlier. I remembered your car from Sunday. Your head was bowed and I thought something was wrong..." Mike's voice trailed off.

"I was just saying my morning prayers."

"You pray every morning?" He couldn't stop the question from escaping.

Rayna smiled, nodding her head. "Every morning. Some people drink coffee to come alive in the morning. I say my prayers," she stated happily, as if she had just won the lottery.

"Please don't take this the wrong way, but you don't look like a believer."

Mike's outlandish comment stilled Rayna. She turned, facing Mike.

"Tell me, Counselor, how does a believer look?" Rayna narrowed her eyes and folded her arms, waiting.

"I mean you're beautiful." Mike grinned, as if that explained everything. Rayna's stare hardened. "I mean in my experience, beautiful women can be vain... I mean, you're not. You're beautiful but not vain." He was floundering. At Rayna's piercing stare, Mike threw up both hands in surrender. "Okay, I'm going to plead the Fifth." Rayna laughed.

"I'm going to let that inane comment pass. Because, as the son of a preacher, I know you wouldn't dare judge anyone based on their looks." Mike felt the censure and owned up to it. "However, let me offer you some advice, Counselor." Rayna walked closer to Mike. "Do not always look on the outside of a person. People can be like mirages. It's the inside of a person that matters." She stepped back and smiled. "You dig?"

Mike nodded his head, thinking this little spitfire had definitely put him in his place. He wondered what Sheila's personality was like. If it was anything like her friend's, he was going to have his work cut out for him. Oddly enough, he was looking forward to it.

"I dig." Mike bowed old world style. "Understood, Counselor. Please forgive my gaffe. I truly meant no harm."

Rayna smiled, sensing he was being truthful with her. She suddenly realized she actually liked Mike. Oh, she did not miss the exchanged looks between him and Sheila. There was definitely something there. It was a tiny seed that needed watering. She prayed that Sheila would water it. She deserved someone great in her life.

Rayna glanced down at her watch. "We had better get going. We don't want you to be late, newbie." Mike smiled at the tease of being the new guy.

"Now, we can't have that, can we?" Mike waved a hand, indicating Rayna should go first. She nodded, leading the way. Together they entered the building. Neither of them saw the dark figure watching them a few feet away.

"Soon, real soon," the figure mumbled.

* * *

The day started out unusually busy, but Mike managed to

take it all in stride. He'd long since surrendered trying to memorize faces to name. It was too daunting a task.

After parting ways with Rayna, he immediately tackled the case he had been given last week. He would be representing a teen who was accused of robbery. After looking over the case and interviewing witnesses, Mike felt confident his client was innocent. It was a case of being at the wrong place at the wrong time. He rubbed at the crick in his neck. Standing, he went to look out his window. He had a great view. It overlooked the park.

The sun was shining, and the park was filled with occupants. Skaters were whizzing by, oblivious to the joggers. Mothers were happily pushing strollers. Dog walkers were using their pooper-scoopers in intervals. Vendors were smiling, working frantically to take orders from the long line of patronages. Mike smiled. For the first time in years, he felt truly alive. He had been a dead man walking, performing mundane tasks by rote and not by purpose. It was a new day, and he was grateful to be alive.

"Well, well, you're certainly living high in the land of the living. Gravy is rolling off your plate." Mike stiffened, recognizing the voice of his childhood friend, Eric.

Without turning around, Mike spoke. "I was always a man of quality. I always believed a man should live according to his true character. When you want something bad enough, it can control you." Mike watched his friend's reflection through the window. "Discipline can be a great teacher. It teaches you control, my friend," he said.

"I can see you've disciplined and controlled your way to the ladder of success. Success looks good on you, man," Eric said.

Mike turned, brown eyes meeting hazel eyes. It was like a dance. Simultaneously, both men approached each other, never breaking eye contact.

"It's been awhile, Montgomery," Eric said.

"It was time for me to return home."

"I'm glad you've returned. Your mug was sorely missed around here. And that twin of yours has become a wimp on the court since he became the family guy." Mike laughed. The two men embraced briefly.

"Have a seat, man. What brings you here?" Eric occupied one of the plush seats in front of Mike.

"I do PI work for your firm from time to time. I'd just rounded out a meeting with a client, when I heard about the new guy; whose name by the way, happened to be the same as one my best friends." Mike heard the subtle rebuke in his friend's voice. He humbly accepted it. "I decided to see if it was my friend of old. To my delight and surprise it was."

Mike watched as his friend leaned back casually, crossing his legs. He wasn't fooled by Eric's display of coolness. Eric uncrossed his legs and leaned forward. His friend was a highly trained human deadly weapon. He hailed from a military background. His father and grandfather were both part of the Special Operation, so it was quite natural for Eric to follow in their steps.

"Eric, I was going to get in contact with you, it's just that the timing was off," Mike said.

"Ah, again the word time, all in the span of ten minutes. Sounds to me, my friend, you're still seeking and not finding." Mike frowned.

Eric leaned forward, bracing both elbows on his knees. Neither man blinked. Eric always called it as he saw it. That was a quality Mike and Bryan most admired about him. But at this moment, Mike didn't care too much for it.

"You know what I'm finding?" Mike looked at his Movado watch. "I'm finding that I'm hungry, and would like to apologize to my boy over lunch."

"It's going to take more than lunch to make up for lost time, Montgomery." Eric stretched the word time for effect. "But it's a start."

"I know, man, I know. I have a lot to make up for. I see now that my decision affected my family as well. Hurt blinded me." Mike leaned back in his seat, absently twirling a Lanier fountain pen. "I just didn't know what to do after the accident. I couldn't stand the looks of friends and family. I didn't know if they pitied me or blamed me. It took a toll on me mentally, and I didn't know what else to do but leave."

"I know you've heard this a thousand times before, but this time I hope it penetrates into your head. It was not…was never your fault." Mike looked at his friend steadily, trying not to give in to the emotions running rampant inside of him. Guilt was in first place. They grew silent. Each man lost in his own thoughts. Eric cleared his throat.

"I haven't given up looking for clues leading to your accident. I'm going to solve this and put the ghost to rest. I wanted to talk to you for awhile now. I found out some interesting things." Mike kept his eyes on Eric's face, trying to fetter out the truth from his facial expression. He revealed nothing.

"What did you find?" Mike asked.

"I'm still following up on some things. I want this to be an airtight case, with no bubbles escaping. Because if my findings match my suspicions…" Eric allowed his words to trail off. "Mike, prepare yourself for what I'm about to tell you, because it's ugly."

Mike felt chilled. Eric's demeanor had become still, indicative that he wasn't going to like what he had to tell him.

"Tell me," Mike said.

Sighing Eric rubbed the bridge of his nose. "I don't think your accident was an accident. It looked as though you were being followed that night. Whoever attacked you didn't randomly select you. You and your wife were a target."

Mike leaned back in his chair stunned, his mind trying to process what Eric just told him. His wife and child's death wasn't a random act of violence. Then why?

"Why us? Who would want to harm me and my family?" Mike stood, too wired to sit. He began pacing around his office. He could barely get the words out. Eric pulled out a small writing pad, and flipped through a couple of pages before stopping. His eyes quickly scanned over the words recorded on the page.

LOVE FOUND ME

"There was a waitress on duty that night. Her name is Patricia. She was just clocking in that night; she was late because she and her fiancé had a huge argument. She remembered seeing a young couple exiting the restaurant, looking very much in love. She said that she watched you and your wife walk to the car, and was awed when you opened the car door for her. When you pulled off, another car immediately pulled off behind you. She claimed that she wouldn't have thought anything about it, but the car was black with dark windows. She remembered getting chills just looking at it."

Mike numbly walked to the window. He took a deep breath and let it out, forcing down a strong sense of anger.

"Did you have any enemies at the time? Owe anyone any money?" Eric asked.

Mike shook his head in the negative. An image of his wife's face flashed across his mind, and he immediately closed his eyes against the pain. Returning to his desk, he fell heavily into his seat.

"At the time, my brother and I had made some very lucrative investments, Eric. They panned out. We're both financially stable for life." Mike smiled. "We've even convinced Pop to make a couple of sound investments."

"Pops took the risk of investing his money? Man, tell me, does he still think we don't know about his secret cash hideaway?" Mike flashed a small grin at Eric.

The boys had discovered by accident that his father had built a small hidden compartment under their parents' bed. They had been playing cops and robber all day. Bryan was the robber, and Mike and Eric were the cops. Bryan had been hiding under their parents' bed when his eyes discovered Fort Knox. It was a small chest filled with a wad of money. When Mrs. Montgomery called them for dinner, they replaced the money back in its hiding place. They never told Pops or anyone else about their find. It was their secret to keep. That is until Pops deemed fit to share it with them.

"Yeah, he still hides it under their bed," Mike said laughing.

"I bet that is one comfortable bed," Eric teased.

"Yes it is. My parents will be comfortable for life." Mike was glad for the change of topic, but knew he had to deal with this latest development. "I can't believe someone intentionally set out to harm my family, man." His eyes blazed with anger. The thought was sickening to him. Before Eric could respond, Rayna walked in.

"Hey, newbie, want to go and grab a bite to eat with me?" she asked.

Mike cleared his throat, trying to reign in his emotions. "Hey, Rayna let me introduce you to a friend of mine. Eric Miller, please meet Rayna Peterson."

Eric stood slowly, his unique eyes never leaving Rayna's face. She looked as though she'd just come from a fashion shoot. She was wearing a plum two-piece pantsuit. Her long hair was in an elegant bun, accentuating her high cheekbones, long curly tendrils escaping. Her feet were clad in sensible black two-inch work shoes. She wore little make up, she had natural beauty. Eric thought she looked refreshingly beautiful. Rayna was stunned, but quickly recovered. Facing Eric, she nodded her head in acknowledgement.

"It's a pleasure to meet you, Mr. Miller," Rayna said.

Eric nodded, his eyes never leaving her face. Rayna's breath hitched under his intense look. She felt as though he were looking right through her. Past all the invisible barriers she'd resurrected. His presence dominated the whole office. That alone said something, as Mike's office was of considerable size. She was suddenly overwhelmed with the need to run. She never ran from anything, she always confronted her issues.

Rayna turned to Mike. "Uh, I see you're busy, so let's take a rain check on that lunch."

Eric stirred immediately, going from stillness to moving muscles, reminding her of a caged tiger. Without waiting for a response, Rayna turned on her heels, quickly exiting the office.

"Wow that was strange." Mike shrugged one broad shoulder. "Come on, man, I'm starving. We still have to talk. Not to mention we have a lot to catch up on."

"I don't think we can cover much in an hour," Eric said.

Mike clasped Eric on the back, exiting the office. Mike was beginning to doubt himself. Was he ready to face his past? Well, ready or not, he wouldn't run anymore.

Eric was calm on the outside, but on the inside, where it matter the most, he was shaken. Never in his life had he ever been affected by the presence of another human being. He didn't like it. He resolved to put as much space between Rayna and himself as possible. He didn't need any distractions. Now if only his heart would obey his mind's command.

Chapter 6

Sheila was pleased at the stack of volunteer applications she was reviewing. The Mending Heart had placed several articles in the local newspaper, asking for volunteers. Their training program was over forty hours of crisis intervention procedures on providing advocacy to victims.

"Sheila, you have a new applicant." Tonya, Sheila's secretary's voice came from the speaker.

"Thanks, Tonya. I will be there in a minute." Sheila mentally shook herself. Normally, she would have Tonya escort her clients in, but her day had started out in a peculiar way. She had a series of unfortunate events happen.

First, she burned her breakfast of toast and cheese omelet. Something she had never done. Secondly, she ran a red light, nearly causing an accident, and spilling her hot cup of cappuccino on her new white blouse. Sheila could not understand what was happening. Yes, she could. Her attention was off kilter, and it was all because of him. She could not get him out of her mind. His eyes, his voice, his words, his presence. The combination was discombobulating to her.

"Arggh, enough of this." A man of Mike's caliber doesn't remember girls like her. She wasn't even in his league. He was rock n' roll and she was country. Sheila smiled at the corny line.

Adding fuel to the fire was the fact that one of the women at the shelter husband was suing her for custody of their two children. He came from money. One thing she learned since working as an advocate was money had a major influence on people. He didn't want the children; it was a power move on his part. He wanted to still have power over his wife. What better way to do it than to use the one thing near and dear...the children. Sheila couldn't understand how people could be so heartless. Physically and mentally abusing women and children was just disgusting. She would do everything in her power to help Mrs. Harper.

LOVE FOUND ME

The Mending Heart was a private not-for-profit organization. Their mission statement is to provide a safe and supportive environment, where domestic victims can get the help they needed to rebuild their lives. It was formed twenty years ago by Amelia Heart, who too was a victim of domestic violence.

The Mending Heart started out in a four-bedroom apartment. It has morphed into a complete service program, housing more than 250 battered women and children in the community. Sometimes, the task seemed overwhelming, as there were more applicants than there were rooms. Sheila mentally shook herself, stood and went to greet her client.

When Sheila reached the reception area, she noticed a small figure in the corner. A cap covered her hair, and she was wearing a long black trench coat, even though it was eighty-five degrees outside. *She must be burning up*, Sheila thought. The woman looked to be in her early twenties. Her brown skin was blotchy and her lips chapped.

"Are you Ms. Lawson?" the woman asked.

"Yes I am. Please follow me." Sheila stopped by her secretary's desk. "Please hold all my calls."

"Yes, Ms. Lawson." Tonya was casting worried glances between the two women.

Sheila smiled at her secretary in reassurance. She motioned for her new applicant to follow her to her office. After they were both seated, Sheila placed her glasses on and smiled. She immediately went into question mode. She fired out the necessary questions without looking up. Are you married? Do you want anyone to know your whereabouts?

"We offer safety up to six weeks of admittance. This time is to seek you a suitable, safe and permanent living arrangement. It saddens me to say this; but most who leave this facility often return back to their assailants. I am not a judge, and I take you at your word," Sheila said.

She continued to look down at her paperwork, occasionally writing something down. She knew this speech by heart. Every time she said it to an applicant, her heart accelerated. Tough love is risky when dealing with abuse. She found she had to be tough to show the seriousness of the situations to these ladies. Despite the beatings and numerous near death experiences, there were always those women who returned to their abusers, only to never see the light of day again.

"If you want help, I'll do everything in my power to give it to you. If you don't want help and are here to waste my time, then don't bother. I believe in wasting not and wanting not." Sheila finally looked up at the young woman. "Now, how may I help you...uh, Ms.?" She allowed her voice to trail off, hoping the woman would supply her name.

"I don't want to be treated textbook style. I'm a real person, with a very real problem."

The woman's voice was raspy. Sheila blinked at the saucy retort. That was definitely not the response she had been expecting.

Clearing her throat, Sheila tried to apologize. "I'm sorry if I offended you, it certainly was not my intent."

The woman stood, simply staring. Sheila thought she was going to leave. Then the woman smiled and nodded her head.

"I'm sorry, Ms. Lawson. I've been handled by the system for so long, that I tend to pass judgment on everyone." The woman walked toward the window. Sheila could see the varied emotions crossing her face. "I'm tired. I never thought I would be reduced to this." She leaned her head against the window, shaking it back and forth.

"Talk to me. How can I help you?" Sheila asked.

"It's hard for me to wake up in the morning. I think to myself, *what's the purpose?* Another day of pain, another day of trying to blend into society. I don't know what it's like to celebrate Thanksgiving or Christmas. I don't even know when my birthday is." The woman laughed bitterly. "I've tried several times to kill myself. I failed at that too. The last time I tried to kill myself, I cut my wrists." Extending her hands, she faced Sheila. Sheila flinched at the jagged six-inch cuts. They were old, but the flesh was still puckered up. "I woke up in the hospital to the news that I would live. That I must live because I was with child." The woman opened her coat, revealing she was swollen with child.

Sheila was frozen. Not because of the woman's pregnancy. She had women seeking shelter all the time who were pregnant or had kids. There was something frighteningly compelling about this woman. There was a dark sadness surrounding her. Sheila's gut screamed for her to distance herself from this woman. Yet, she felt compelled to help her and her unborn child. Finally moving, the young woman returned to her seat.

"That was a stupid move on my part, I realize that now." She looked directly at Sheila. "I'm not crazy. What I am is tired. I'm tired of being a victim. I'm tired of feeling helpless. I can't do this alone. My baby and I need help. I want to live." She pointed to her chest and began to pound on it. "I want to live. I want to live. I want to live," she kept saying over and over.

Sheila felt chilled. She couldn't put her finger on it, but something was definitely off kilter. She knew whatever it was; it had something to do with the young woman before her. From the moment the woman entered her office, she knew her life had suddenly changed forever.

"You've made the right step by coming here. I want to help you, but we have to follow protocol and procedures here," Sheila said.

"I want to live," was the repeated soft reply.

"Please tell me your name." Sheila felt her heart constrict at the declaration. "I'm going to do everything in my power to see that happens for you, I promise."

The woman held Sheila's eyes, after awhile a small smile formed on her lips. "Monica. Monica Henry is my name."

"Alright, Monica, we're making progress. How old are you? Where do you live?"

"I'm twenty-four and I live in hell." Her eyes hardened at the declaration.

"Well, your address is about to change," Sheila vowed. She

meant it. She would do all within her power to help this stranger and her child. "Monica, we must follow protocol. By that I mean I need some information. Then you will be assigned a caseworker to help you regain your life back."

"Yes. Well, how very routine of you," came the sarcastic reply. Monica slowly leaned back in her chair, her face hardening.

Sheila's gaze landed on Monica's left hand. She kept rubbing something as if it was soothing her. Sheila briefly wondered what it was. Was it a good luck charm? Monica smiled bitterly.

"Stupid, stupid me. I honestly thought you were one of the good ones. Someone I could confide in and that *you*," she paused to emphasize the word you, "would certainly help me. Yet you choose to pass me along like a pair of used shoes. I thought you were..." Monica voiced trailed off.

Sheila's brows rose in curiosity. She wondered what Monica was going to say. Monica folded her arms under her breasts.

"Look, I'm tired and hungry. Are you giving me shelter or not?" Sheila looked into weary sad eyes, and could not help but wonder what were the events that caused her life to take the direction it had.

"Yes, Monica. You will have shelter tonight. You'll be safe," Sheila said.

Monica shook her head. "I can't remember ever feeling safe. I'm starting to believe that there is no such thing." She held up her hand when Sheila started to speak. "Please don't. Maybe there is a place of safety, but not for me. I have experienced too many tragedies to believe such a place exists."

"Tell me," Sheila encouraged.

"One day maybe, however, not today. I really am tired," Monica said wearily.

Sheila pressed the intercom. When her secretary answered, she gave instructions to prepare housing accommodations for Monica. "Please tell Mrs. Howard to contact Dr. Mallory. We need to set up a physical for Ms. Henry. I would feel comfortable if she and her baby were examined." Sheila disconnected.

"Thank you," Monica said.

"You're welcome." Sheila wished that it was that easy, but something on the inside was telling her there was something Monica wasn't telling her. Lately, she'd been having the feeling that something bad was going to happen. Something was on the horizon waiting to make its move. She couldn't pinpoint exactly what it was, but she sensed it had something to do with her new applicant.

They continued on for the next thirty minutes. Monica agreed to meet Sheila at the safe house early tomorrow morning. For more than the first time that day, Sheila prayed she was doing the right thing.

VANESSA RICHARDSON

Chapter 7

Inhaling the fresh crisp air confirmed that she had made the right decision. The song *I Need Some Me Time,* by Heather Headley played softly from her portable radio. Looking around, Sheila mentally checked off all her items. She had her small canvas, paintbrushes, her array of paints, and her black chalk. The park was not busy this early in the morning, which was why she chose the time. She wanted to be inspired and needed a few distractions. Already, her muses where speaking to her.

Across the pond, she saw a couple. They were beatific. The woman had dreadlocks that flowed down to her waist. The man wore small twists. Both were dressed in African garb. The colors were majestic. Sheila's hands took on a life of their own. Soon, she was caught up in the frenzy.

Time faded, hunger faded, noises faded. The images in her head were bold and clear. They were adamant, wanting to come alive. Slender fingers glided across the canvas. Her heart rate accelerated, as the images started to come alive. The couple started to walk away. That was okay; because her mind had already locked down the pose she wanted from them.

"Wow that is wonderful." That voice! She knew its owner. Sheila glanced up into familiar eyes, and immediately felt the same jolt which had hit her in church. "I'm sorry. I hope I'm not distracting you." Mike looked at the unfinished painting. He was very impressed at what he saw. Sheila was a fantastic artist. He felt very proud of her talent. "Sheila, have you had any formal training?"

"No. At one point, I wanted to go to art school to sharpen my skills, but the timing never seemed right," she said, with a small shrug.

Mike wasn't fooled. He sensed if given the chance, Sheila would have pursued her passion of painting. "I have a friend who is an artist, and know that when an idea hits him, he has to do his thing…" His voice trailed off.

LOVE FOUND ME

Mike was horrified. He could not believe he was blubbering like an idiot. Sheila was just staring at him with those beautiful brown eyes of hers.

It was a peculiar day. Rising early, Mike felt the compulsion to jog in the park. Normally, he slept late on Saturdays. After completing his run, while he was stretching, he looked up and saw his lady. That was what she came to be in his head... his lady. He found comfort in that.

Sheila was speechless. Something about this man captured her heart. But how could that be? It was his eyes; she reasoned. The way he was looking at her, as if he was asking something of her, and her heart was responding. Silly girl, men like Mike were not interested in women like her.

"No, you didn't make me lose focus. I was just doing a preliminary sketch, and was going to complete it at home." Sheila wanted to run; but he was making her feel, with just a glance, innocuous.

Sensing she was about to leave, desperately Mike searched for a reason to delay her exit. "Are you an artist by profession or pleasure?" Lame perhaps, but that was all he had.

Feeling safe with the topic of art, Sheila answered, "Pleasure. I'm a Domestic Violence Counselor. Painting is my release mechanism."

"You're really quite good at it. May I?" Mike asked, pointing to her unfinished drawing.

"It isn't finished and..." Sheila felt herself panicking. She was a closet painter. Sharing her creations with the public was frightening; but sharing it with this man was sending her emotions off the Richter scale. Honestly, her mouth formed the denial, but those eyes again, darn it. How could she deny him anything when he looked at her like that? Did he know the havoc he was creating upon her emotions?

She could smell his aftershave, mingled with his sweat, and had to fight the impulse to lean into him. His shoulders looked so strong and sturdy; she wanted to rest her head upon them. She was tired of carrying the weight all by herself. For once, she would love to know what it was like to share her world with someone you loved.

Mike sat next to Sheila on the bench, who immediately stiffened at his close proximity. This was too much; her senses were going into overload. She had to beat it like Michael Jackson, because this man was definitely a thriller to her system. He allowed his eyes to remain focused on the couple Sheila had painted on the canvas. Mike smiled.

"You have captured their essence perfectly. It seems so life like." He felt himself getting excited as an idea began to germinate. "Have you ever considered putting your paintings on display?"

Sheila was shocked by the question. "On display? You do mean for people to look at?" Fear caused her voice to raise a couple of octaves.

Still eyeing the painting, Mike nodded excitedly. *His lady was beautiful and talented.* The painting only ignited the craving to get to know her on every level, and he meant every level.

Sheila, seeing that Mike was serious, could only stare at him. He finally met her stare, and her heart leaped at their eye connection. Sheila wondered again about their strong chemistry together. *The connection was deeper*, she thought. Mike touched her soul. She made a mental note to call Rayna and ask if such a thing possible. Sheila was clueless when it came to relationships. For so long, she hid herself in her work helping others, when she really needed helping herself.

"My friend owns an art gallery in Buckhead, and every year he hosts an art extravaganza that displays local up and coming artists. By looking at this painting I'd definitely say you'd be a perfect featured artist, Sheila." Mike liked saying her name.

Sheila found she liked hearing Mike say her name.

"That is too big of a step for me, Mike. I don't think so. I mean, who would be interested in my paintings?" Sheila leaped up, turning to face Mike. "You really think I'm that good?" she asked, nibbling nervously on her lips.

"No, Sheila, I think you are better than good. I know my friend would definitely be interested in showcasing you. If anything, it would be for receiving credit for discovering you."

"What is your friend's name?" she asked.

"Earl Jones."

"*The* Earl Jones?" Sheila asked, in wide-eyed wonderment. "The Earl Jones whose paintings have been featured on *Live from Atlanta*? His paintings are the most sought after by Hollywood's A list celebrities." She set back down next to Mike.

"Yes, the one and only," Mike said. A vendor walked by, and the smell of hot dogs awoke hunger pangs in Sheila. "I think its lunchtime," he said, smiling.

Sheila glanced at her watch in shock. "I had no idea it was so late. When I paint, time can become illusive to me." Patting her flat stomach, she stood to her feet. Mike reached to assist her, and was shocked by the potent current that ran through him. Did she feel that? A wide-eyed, Sheila leaped back in shock. *Yes, she felt it too*, Mike thought.

He didn't know what was happening between him and Sheila, it seemed almost magical. One thing for sure, he wasn't about to let it go. Sheila quickly gathered her things, attempting to go around Mike, who blocked her exit.

"Please let me treat you to lunch. It's the least I can do, seeing how I interrupted your focus and all. Plus, I'd like to try to convince you to showcase your painting. Don't rob the world of such great talent, Sheila."

Mike could feel himself growing anxious. He sounded desperate, even to his ears. He knew he looked like a stalker in her eyes, but he couldn't help it. His instincts were screaming at him to fight for this woman. Moreover, he was definitely fighting an inward battle. Was he ready for another relationship? Could he be the man that she needed? *God, lead me on what to say to this woman. My heart is calling out to her. Could she be the one?*

If Sheila was aware of the inward battle Mike was having, she didn't show it. He noticed her trademark of tilting of her head to the side, followed by her beatific smile. *Two lethal combinations,* Mike thought. He was mesmerized by this woman. She held the sun in her eyes.

"Okay, Mike. I got to tell you right now I'm in the mood for something greasy," Sheila said.

Releasing his breath, Mike laughed. She just helped him and did not even know it. He glanced down at her slender frame. She didn't look to be 125 pounds soaking wet.

Sheila discerning Mike's thought smiled. "Rule number one, Mike; never judge a woman by her size," she said.

Her words reminded Mike of his similar conversation with Rayna about judging a woman. Man, was he out of the loop when it came to the fairer sex. He had limited experience with the dating scene. He married young. He and his wife were childhood friends. Growing up, they were always verbally open with each other, meaning they said just about anything to each other. After she died, he really had no interest to date anyone. No one had captured his attention until now.

A breeze disturbed Sheila's orderly tresses. Without hesitation, Mike reached out and restored the soft lock. It felt as soft as the finest of silks. Time stood still. They stood there in the park surrounded by park occupants, vendors and wayward children. Yet they were oblivious to these happenings. It was just the two of them, each grappling with the past, and weary with the future. A child shrieked in shock as she fell from her bike, bringing them out of their hypnotic moment. Mike reached for Sheila's tote, and escorted her to his Silver BMW.

"If you don't mind, I would like to drive my car." Sheila didn't think she was ready to ride alone with him just yet. His presence was heady, and she was not ready for heady. *Lord, why now? Why this man?* When Mike looked at her, it was as if she found the answer. But in actuality she had no answers, she was still seeking answers.

Feeling herself panicking, she started to cancel the lunch date, but made the huge mistake of looking up into his eyes. Really now, how could she to say no to him when he used those weapons of destruction? For that is what he was going to do, destroy her carefully erected wall to her heart, and then where will she be? Back at the beginning.

"I wouldn't want to inconvenience you. I can follow you." Sheila faltered at Mike's stare.

He braced his legs apart and folded his arms across his chest. He did this more as a preventive measure than anything. He wanted to reach out and pull Sheila into his arms.

"We Montgomery men are raised to be gentlemen, Sheila. Now if my mother would see me do as you've just suggested, trust me, she would be quite displeased with me. I have the fear of Clara Montgomery in me. She has eyes everywhere. She sees and knows all. Matter of fact, I wouldn't be surprised if she wasn't hiding behind one of those trees over there." Mike pointed in the direction of several trees.

Sheila couldn't hold back her laughter. Wow, it felt really good to laugh, to be carefree. She liked that Mike had a sense of humor. It was evident through his humor that he both loved and respected his mother. That was a plus, a woman could tell how a man treated his woman by the way he treated his mother.

"Besides, I want to take advantage of all the time you give me, Sheila."

How could she say no to him? Deep down, she didn't want to. Sheila tilted her head, the sun highlighting her luxurious tresses.

"It's obvious Mrs. Montgomery has raised you right, and I wouldn't want you to deviate from such great training." Mike nodded, eyes twinkling. "So, we'll take your car."

Unlocking the passenger's side door, he assisted Sheila inside. He then placed her painting case and canvas gently in the backseat. Sliding inside the driver's seat, Mike faced Sheila.

"I promise you will be safe with me," he said.

"I don't doubt that." At her words, Mike's eyes searched Sheila's face. He must have found what he was searching for, as he suddenly smiled. "Are we ready then?" Sheila's stomach answered for her. They both laughed. The tension evaporated in the soft winds.

"Yes, I'm ready and very hungry," Sheila said.

Chapter 8

Mike offered up a prayer of thanks. Just this morning, he was thinking about how to subtly ask Sheila out. All ideas had abandoned him; he was never good with words. He was more of a man of action. Now here they were about to break bread together. He hazarded a look in Sheila's direction, and was awarded a smile. His heart accelerated. This was a good sign. She was becoming comfortable with him.

Mike did not allow himself to believe the road to knowing his lady would be an easy one. She was hiding something from him, and he was going to find out what it was. Starting the car, he maneuvered into traffic.

"Do you like jazz?" he asked.

"I love jazz. Coltrane is the man," Sheila answered.

Mike's eyes widened with appreciation. He glanced quickly at her before returning his eyes to the road.

"Great minds think alike. I happen to love Coltrane also. Matter of fact, I happened to be his greatest fan. There isn't anything I don't know about the man." Mike pressed the play button, and the melodic sound of *Afro Blue* filled the air.

Sheila turned toward Mike, folding her arms. "Is that right? John Coltrane is from the south; but where was he born?"

"Ahh, that is too elementary a question, my dear Watson." Mike laughed at Sheila's mock look of outrage. "John William Coltrane was born on September 23, 1926 in Hamlet, North Carolina. It's sad how he is rarely mentioned in some prominent books on jazz, even though legendary greats, with much due respect to them, Miles Davis and Louis Armstrong are listed up to twenty times. Coltrane's technique for using syncopation in his music was pure genius on his part." Mike beamed.

They rode in comfort, silently allowing the music to wash over them. Sheila slid further down into her seat, smiling in appreciation. She couldn't recall ever feeling so safe and appreciated. Immediately, her artistic mind began to form images to Coltrane's soothing melodic sound.

She and Mike were strolling down the beach holding hands. The sun was setting. Mike suddenly stopped them, and turned Sheila in the direction of the fading sun. She looked at the red orange ball, and was awed by one of God's creations. It amazed her that with every rising and going down of the sun, presented another opportunity to live and be happy. A sigh of contentment escaped her as she leaned back into Mike's embrace. He tightened his arms around her, holding her as if she was as valuable as a diamond ring. The moment was beatific.

Smiling, Sheila slowly opened her eyes; and tilted her head to silently examine Mike. He was so handsome. He looked relaxed, and he was smiling. As if sensing her silent perusal of him, he suddenly turned to her and smiled. Sheila's heart melted.

"I love walking along the beach. I absolutely adore watching the sunset," Sheila said.

Mike wanted to know what was on her mind. He didn't want to have to guess at it. He wanted her to share with him her feelings and thoughts. He knew she had questions and doubts, and the fact that she was willing to set aside her fears for him was humbling. He was curious about where the conversation was going, so he remained silent, waiting for Sheila to continue.

She swallowed hard, tears burning behind her lids.

"When I was a little girl; I couldn't wait for night to fall. In the stillness of the night, I found peace. While everyone else was sleeping, and the group home was quiet, I could just be me. I never felt like I belonged anywhere or to anyone." Pausing, she turned and looked out the window.

Mike's grip tightened on the wheel. He had to restrain himself from pulling over on the side of the road to hold Sheila. The man in him wanted to take her pain away, ridding her of past hurtful memories, and replacing them with new and loving memories of them happy and starting a family together. He couldn't imagine himself growing up without a family. He thought of his parents and brother, and said a prayer a thanks.

Sheila nibbled on her bottom lip. Mike smiled. He was becoming familiar with her patterns now. She often nibbled on her bottom lip when she was nervous, and blinked rapidly when scared.

"In the day, I had to put on my strong armor. I tried blending in, to act as normal as possible. It was hard work trying to cover the hole in my heart. As young as I was, I knew something was missing." Sheila lifted her hand, absently outlining circles on the car window. "With each sunset, I found myself grateful for just surviving another day. That was what I was doing really, surviving, not living. Everything was done by rote. Wake up, wash and get dressed. Attend classes. Complete chores. Then wait for the peace of night." Dropping her hand, she allowed her eyes to finally rest on Mike. Her long lashes were spiked with tears. "I'm ready to live. I want to belong. There is no difference in being alone and not belonging to someone. They both hurt."

Mike felt his love for her coursing through him like molten lava flowing from a volcano. He was at a loss for words. He wanted to tell her that she would never have to experience being alone again. His parents and brother would welcome her with open arms. He wanted to tell her that she did belong with him. He didn't think Sheila was ready to hear all of that just yet. So he did what he wanted to do since first seeing her at church. He reached out and took Sheila's hand into his own.

"You will live, and you will belong. That you survived isolation as a child and still came out better and not bitter is a testament of your strength. Many people would have deviated from the path of right. Doing unsavory things." Mike squeezed Sheila's hand softly, and she squeezed his back. "Sheila, baby, I don't know what the future holds for us. I just know that at this moment right now, I accept what is happening between us. My past has kept me from living for so long. I'm ready to live again. Timing is funny, life is funny. This right here, what we got is right."

Mike spoke with such fierceness that it brought a lump to Sheila's throat. She could only nod in the affirmative. She was ready to live, and prayed that he would have a place in her future. She not only wanted Mike to be a permanent fixture in her life, she needed him to be. He was a source of comfort. He was self-sacrificing, and was willing to show his vulnerability to her. All these qualities were exceptional, but it was his faith that had endeared him to her. He had her heart in his hands. Now, could she tell him this?

Chapter 9

She was in a battle, and was losing the fight. She was no match against Mother Nature. The wind and rain was tag teaming against her. She was freezing wet. Her mother often chastised her for always making haste decisions.

Rayna grunted as the phrase "mama knows best" entered her mind. Her self-confession made her irate. At the age of thirty-four, she was forced to admit that her mother's observant truths concerning her only daughter were true. Rayna had a bad tendency to leap before looking. Today, she leaped again, and without looking, and was paying the piper for it too.

As the strong wind brutally tossed her around like loose debris, she heard the sound of a vehicle approaching and stiffened.

Rayna murmured, "Just great. It might be some deranged stalker who picks up innocent freezing wet women." The rain was making it hard for her to see. She had tripped several times over the fallen debris. Her teeth were beginning to chatter from the cold. *Was the rain ever going to cease?* It seemed like it had been raining for hours now.

"Excuse me? Are you stranded? I can give you a ride, if you like," a voice from behind her asked.

Rayna, murmuring softly under her breath, she tripped, caught herself and kept on walking.

"Look, you're soaking wet. This isn't the type of weather one should be walking in."

Silence

"Look, you can use my cell to call someone if you're concerned about my abducting you." The stranger's concerned words finally penetrated through to Rayna.

"No, I'm fine. Just fine, thank you," Rayna called out, quickening her steps. *Oh, God, he was a stalker who preyed on young women. Soaking wet women, who had no business being out alone in the pouring rain,* she chastised herself. The car continued to follow. *God, please, if You get me out of this mess, I promise to call my mother and confess all the bad things I've done as a child.*

Lightning lit the sky, followed by the booming sound of thunder. Rayna screamed, tripping again over fallen debris. Landing flat on her stomach in the pouring rain, she laid there stunned. It was too much. Her falling again in the storm was the last straw. The dam of false strength she had erected for so many years had broken. Like a tsunami, her tears of hurt flowed. She began to cry fast and furiously. From her low position, she looked up at the dark gray sky. The rain continued to pelt at her, the wind continued to pull at her long tresses, and she ignored all these outside interferences. Her heart went into overdrive, as pent up emotions began to surface. In her fury, she began to hit the ground in frustration.

She was angry, angry at her choice of becoming a mother being taken away. The rain continued and she purged herself, finally confessing that she was hurting. She had suffered a setback, but vowed she would make it through her personal storm.

The rain was refreshing. It was washing the fast falling tears from her eyes. Turning over on her back, Rayna closed her eyes. The rain continued to fall, washing her.

A dark shadow fell over her, causing Rayna to scream out. The stalker! How could she have forgotten about the stalker? She turned back over on her stomach and began to crawl away from her would be stalker. She had a problem, but she wanted to live to deal with it.

"Help me! Someone help me!" she screamed.

He had witnessed Rayne's breakdown. His first instinct had been to run to her, but something staid him. He simply watched her. Hurt recognizes hurt. Even in the storm, he saw her hurt. When she cried out, it was all he could do not to get out of his car and wrap her in his arms. He knew the healing process well. The number one key to healing was to release the hurt. Right now, standing over her, he had to make her realize he was not the enemy.

"That is what I'm trying to do, help you. Ms. uh, look, is you certifiably insane?" His voice sounded oddly amused.

Outraged, Rayna stilled. Turning around, she was about to let him have one good lashing before their battle ensued. She froze, because this man was intriguing. He had skin the color of rich mocha. Broad shoulders, enhanced by the black leather jacket he was wearing. His eyes were hazel. Then he smiled, and her heart leaped. Then he moved. Then she moved.

"If you come near me I will use this." She held one hand out defensively.

The stranger looked at the pitiful weapon and laughed. It was one of those deep belly laughs, which made you want to join in, even when you didn't get the joke. She had to bite down hard on her lip to refrain from laughing. This was no laughing matter.

"Yeah, I would definitely say that you are certifiable. Pity you're so beautiful too."

Oh, come on now. Did his voice have to sound so, so…Barry White? It took a moment for the stranger's words to register. She could not believe what he just said. Not the 'certifiable' comment, she would deal with that later. The 'beautiful' comment. Sure, she had been told she was beautiful countless times by men and women, because she was fierce when it came to her appearance.

She wasn't a frivolous person, she was quite frugal actually, but she had an image to live up to as one of Atlanta's most successful attorneys. It was a hard profession, even more so considering she was a woman. Her high-powered suits made her feel in charge. Everything had to be in place. Order was her place of comfort.

However, the compliment coming from this man affected her differently. His words made her proud to be a woman. Not liking the feeling of losing control, she felt herself becoming angry. She was certain she looked like some wet stray off the street. Yet, he claimed to see the beauty in the storm.

He laughed as he witnessed the myriad of emotions crossing Rayna's face. The sound was beatific, causing her stomach to flip flop. Her rescuer gently threw up his hands.

"Look. I promise not to hurt you. I just want to help, that's all. Look, you can come to my car and use my mobile phone to call someone to help you if you like." He nodded at the meager weapon in her hand. "And you can put your weapon away."

Rayna felt her face warming with embarrassment. She quickly put the ballpoint pen in her sweat pants pocket.

"I went jogging and got caught in the storm," she stated, scrambling to her feet. Rayna was so cold, that her teeth were chattering loudly.

"Look, this is ridiculous, you're drenched through and through, and you're freezing. You can catch pneumonia is this weather. Allow me to take you home. If it makes you feel safer, you can even keep your weapon pointed at me." Rayna hugged her arms tightly around herself. "I give you my word that I will not harm you, lady." He waited.

Rayna sighed; it was ridiculous how she got caught in this rainstorm. Maybe he was her hidden blessing in the storm. She sighed again and the stranger smiled. "Oh, all right..." Before she could finish her sentence, he purposely approached her.

Suddenly she felt strong arms around her waist and froze. She felt the zing; its intensity penetrating to the visceral of her being. Did he feel that? Shocked, she looked up into the stranger's eyes, and they too held surprise, confirming he too felt it. Rayna sighed.

"I live a couple blocks away." She glanced down at her wet garb, and said, "I do appreciate your kindness." Rayna leaned back into his embrace.

"Let's get out of this storm," he said.

Rayna was too shocked to protest. Truth be told, she didn't want to. It felt good being carried. This moment was surreal. She felt like a damsel in distress. She smiled, deciding to play the part. *Besides, I'm never going to see my rescuer again, which is a pity*, she thought. He smelled so good, like rain shower and pine. Rayna wrapped her arms around his neck and relaxed. The thought came to her that she seen had him somewhere before.

LOVE FOUND ME

What am I doing, he thought to himself. This whole ridiculous scene felt right; to right. He had been on his way to the gym, and had decided to take a different route, when he saw Rayna jogging. He immediately recognized her. Either she was one heck of an actress, or she had totally forgotten their one meeting.

Eric couldn't understand why Rayna hadn't been hurrying home instead of jogging, as the storm clouds were gathering. He had started to drive away, but something staid him. Then she fell. He watched her. In the end, he wanted her.

Rayna inhaled sharply. When they reached the sleek black Porsche, she knew there was no way she was going to damage something that beautiful, it just wasn't right.

"I'm going to get water all over your seat and mud on your floor. Look, maybe this is a bad idea. I'm already soaked through; I can just run the remaining blocks." Rayna was squirming in his arms.

Eric started to protest, but his words were interrupted as lightning pierced the sky, followed by the loud sound of thunder. Rayna screamed, clinging tightly to her savior, all thoughts of protest forgotten. Besides, the stranger looked like he could afford to have the Porsche cleaned. Thunder sounded again. God was not playing with her today. Rayna vowed to get to church early Sunday morning to repent for the things she has knowingly and unknowingly done.

He just laughed. Opening the passenger side door, he gently placed Rayna inside. Rounding the car, he entered the driver's side, continuing to laugh. If a yawn was contagious maybe laughter was too, because Rayna soon found herself laughing with him. Seriously, one could not help but to laugh at the ridiculousness of the situation.

Her rescuer faced her and smiled. "Where to lady?" he asked.

Sheila swallowed hard at his choice of words. "Murchison Road," she said.

He just stared at her. Rayna wanted to break his hold but couldn't. Again came the feeling that she knew him from somewhere.

Say something, she wanted to scream at him. His hand shot out, moving a wet strand of hair from her eyes. Inhaling sharply, Rayna blinked twice, turning her attention to her folded hands.

"Murchison Road it is then." Turning the key in the ignition, the car purred to life.

The ride was bitter sweet for Rayna. The close confinement of the car enhanced sound and movement. It was still raining outside. Within a matter of minutes, the car had warmed up, defeating an earlier chill. Rayna leaned back. Closing her eyes, she smiled. She felt peace settling over her. Her mystery man reminded her of the earth. His woodsy cologne, mixed with the rain, was a heady combination.

"You know you support my theory that happiness can be gained in the rain." His voice was like a bucket of cold water. "Please don't stop smiling. A smile is a gift that very few people give or want to give, especially in the rain, or should I say in their pain?" he said.

Rayna's eyes remained closed. She wanted to know where this conversation was leading, so she remained still.

"The rain is necessary at times. It's a cleanser. Have you ever noticed that after it rains, the world looks so refreshed? So revived?" He nodded his head. "Yes, the rain is a cleanser."

Rayna finally understood. He'd witnessed her moment of releasing back there. She had released her pent up hurt in the rain, and yes, she felt refreshed. Was he called for a purpose in her life? She wanted to feel embarrassed but could not. Instead, she felt like she had gained a friend. She suddenly was overwhelmed with a need to confide in him.

"Right here," Rayna said, pointing to a moderate-sized two-story home when he turned onto Murchison Road. She was scared that her mystery man would or would not ask for her number. She anxiously waited.

He pulled over to the curb, not cutting the engine off. Rayna unfastened her seatbelt and waited. Nothing. That was her clue.

"Well, thanks for the ride," she said, opening the car door.

He nodded. His car remained revved, indicating he was impatient to leave. Rayna's heart plummeted with rejection and disappointment, which was stupid, considering she had just met him a second ago.

"Thank you so much for rescuing me." She wanted him to do something, but didn't exactly know what. At the thought of never seeing him again, an unexpected sadness washed over her. She felt safe in his presence. He stared. "I had better be going," she said.

Say something, she thought in anguish. He nodded. Swallowing hard, Rayna exited the car; tears pricking her eyelids. Walking up her stairs, she could still hear his car engine running. Like her, it was running from this sudden attraction. She was never an active participant in matters of the heart. She was the one sitting on the sidelines, watching the scenes play out with couples. Her life was more G rated; a 24-hour Nickelodeon marathon.

Hands shaking, Rayna removed her keys from her pocket and opened the door, refusing to look back at the stranger. If she had spared a look, she would have seen him exiting his car, and purposely walking toward her.

Chapter 10

Eric was very close to Rayna when she finally managed to open her door. She hastily entered her abode; firmly closing the door behind her, closing both the world and him out. She never looked back.

He stood there feeling like a first class heel. He knew he had disappointed her. Her eyes had called to him, and he had declined. He knew he had hurt her, but he couldn't become involved with her. No woman would ever be safe with him in their lives. He was a target. He long ago accepted that he would never marry and have a family. Wiping a hand over his face, he sighed. The timing was off.

He felt the soft sprinkling of rain. Yet he remained frozen where he stood. The rain picked up momentum, causing him to seek the shelter of his car. He could still feel her presence inside, the faint smell of flowers still lingered. This was the first indicator that he was in trouble. Shaking his head, he merged into traffic.

Standing in her foyer, Rayna looked around. The house suddenly felt huge and empty. She felt alone. She stood frozen in place, confused by what she was feeling. Locking her door, she looked around at her spacious house through new eyes. It was too big for a single person. When she had first purchased the home, she wanted it for its vastness. The more money she made, the more space she wanted. She felt free. Now she felt alone and empty. The silence was deafening.

Pulling off her coat, she slowly made her way to her bedroom. She looked into the bedroom mirror and flinched. She looked like a drowned cat. *No wonder Mr. Wonderful didn't ask for my number*, she thought. "Arrgh, enough of this. A nice hot bath is what I need," she said aloud.

Turning, she walked into her bathroom. She allowed the hot water to fill her claw-shaped tub, pouring in her favorite vanilla scented bathing gel. She set down on the end of the tub, and was again arrested by her image in the mirror. She walked over to her banjo-shaped countertop and looked at herself, wondering what people saw when they looked at her. People always complimented her on her looks. What they didn't know was that she was highly intelligent. A fact she refused to hide. She believed in having fun with caution. She had kissed many frogs, and had dated many wolves in sheep's clothing. The disappointments proved too great, so she had decided that dating just was not worth the effort. If God wanted her to marry, and she hoped He did, He would send him to her doorstep or something, because she was just sick and tired of being sick and tired.

"I know there is someone out there waiting for me. The question is: where the heck was he at?" Turning around, she shut off the water, her bath was ready.

Divesting herself from her wet clothes, she stepped into the hot scented water. She reflected on her meeting with the stranger, and immediately smiled. She knew she would never forget this day if she lived to be a hundred. Besides, a man who looks like him could not possibly be single. Rayna vowed to put the stranger out of her mind, but that was easier said than done.

After getting out of the tub, she walked into her bedroom, slathered her skin with vanilla oil and retired for the night, taking the memories of Mr. Wonderful with her. Burrowing deep under the soft comforter, she smiled. Closing her eyes, she could still see his face in her mind's eye. The smile returned. His presence was electrical.

The shrilling sound of the phone startled her. She looked at the clock on her nightstand. It was 10 o'clock pm. Who could be calling her at such an hour? All her friends knew she was an early sleeper and early riser. Sheila! Maybe something has happened? Flinging off the comforter, she set on the edge of her bed, and answered the phone.

"Hello," she said, fear causing her voice to rise.

"All dry and comfy, are we?"

Rayna fell off the bed in shock, hitting her elbow on her nightstand in the process. "Ouch!"

"Are you alright? Do you need me?"

It was her Mystery man! How did he get her number?

"I'm coming over there, if you don't answer in the next second, lady."

That spurred movement from Rayna. Rubbing her wounded elbow, she answered, "No, I was just....um shocked to hear from you."

Silence.

Rayna waited. She felt like she should be saying something, but for the life of her, she couldn't think of a thing. She was speechless, utterly speechless. Anyways, he called her; he should be the one talking.

Silence.

Rayna worked her mouth and nothing came out. She began to pace up and down her room. Curling the phone chord around her fingers, she twisted it too tight, and while trying to unwrap it, she broke her nail. Muffling a cry, she flexed her hand up and down. This was too much. Already this man was causing her to lose possession of her faculties. Wait a minute! How did he get her number?

"I know you're wondering how I got your number, right?" Eric asked.

Rayna was speechless. Her mind immediately began to form stories of its own. *Please, Lord, do not let him be a stalker. The one man who causes her to feel alive is a stalker,* she thought. She remembered watching an episode of Oprah about a stalker.

"Your wallet fell out in my car." Eric's voice pulled her out of her self-ranting.

His voice reminded her of rain falling against her windowpane. It was a sound she always found comforting. She felt like a lost part of her was found. His voice was soothing; it wasn't heavy or high-pitched. It was just right. She glanced at the fireplace in her room. She wanted to light it and listen to him talk for days. She felt safe in his presence.

"I found your driver's license, dialed information, and was given your number." Eric didn't mention his information came from his connection of a friend from the CIA. Rayna didn't know what to say so she remained silent. "I know it sounds contrived, but it is a true story." There was a hint of laughter in his voice. Rayna smiled. Total brain function was returning to her.

"Thank you, uh..."

"Eric. Eric Miller" He waited to see if she would recognize his name.

"Thank you, Mr. Miller.

"Eric." His voiced was laced with a hint of command. He was a little miffed that she still seemed to not recognize him. It was a little insulting to his male ego.

Rayna felt goose bumps sprinkling her skin. Not good. She was determined to stay in control of the situation. Using her courtroom voice, the one that made criminals cringe and lawyers respect her, said, "Mr. Miller," she intentionally used his last name again, "it was very gracious of you to see me home. I made a bad judgment call. One that may cost me a trip to my family doctor, but only time will tell...

A strange noise assaulted her ears. Rayna stood shocked, realizing that he was laughing at her. This irked her somehow.

"Mr. Miller, I fail to see the humor you're displaying. But as it stands now, I can use a good laugh, so please do share."

"You. You're funny," he replied softly. "You're trying so hard to show me someone you're not. There is a saying, that like recognizes like. I recognize you, lady." Rayna's heart leaped at the endearment. "Look, Rayna, I don't play games. I know what type of man I am, and I make no excuses for it. I know that something happened today between you and me, and quite frankly, it has scared the hell out of me."

"Excuse me? Mr. Miller..."

"Eric," he commanded. Rayna looked outside her window. The rain had ceased. "Say my name. It won't hurt to do so, lady."

Sighing, she placed a dainty hand against the window. The sky sparkled with unnumbered stars. She wanted to reach out and capture one, place it in a jar, and let its light shine. She wanted happiness.

"Eric, today was an unusual day for me. I promise you, I don't normally head out into contending weather. I don't fall on the ground, releasing my frustrations for the world to see, and I don't accept rides from complete strangers."

"You know what is funny?" The day started of strange for me as well. I was not supposed to be on that part of town, today. Something compelled me to drive that way. I am glad that I followed my instincts." Eric's voiced lowered. "I've just met you, and already I can't get you out of my mind." He chuckled softly, the deep sound causing Rayna's heart to leap in response. Eric rubbed the bridge of his nose. "Funny, I'm intrigued by a beautiful...and possibly certifiable woman. And if such is my fate, then I have no other choice but to embrace it."

For the second time that night, Rayna was shocked. She was amazed by the crazy dialogue taking place between her and Eric. Not knowing how to respond, she simply listened.

"Rayna, I don't play games. When I see something I want, I go after it. If I want it bad enough, I'm determined that eventually it will become mine. Remember these words of fact I'm about to state to you, lady. I take care of what's mine, always have, and always will."

Rayna dropped down on the mattress, desperately in need of some grapefruit juice. If she were not a God-fearing woman, she would be drinking something much stronger.

"I think I have said enough for tonight. Sleep well, Rayna," Eric said.

Rayna was suddenly overwhelmed. She wanted to know what he was thinking. Where was he at at that moment?

"In the storm, I saw something in you," Eric whispered. "I want to get to know you. You have no idea how much," he said, blowing out a breath. "But the timing; this thing between us can't be," he said sadly.

Rayna felt like someone had just punched her in the stomach. Was she dreaming? She was up one minute and down the next. It was time to take control of the situation.

"Look, Eric, I'm not asking you, a stranger at that, for anything. I'm in a busy place in my life right now, and a relationship factors nowhere in it. So, be at ease. Thank you for the ride and conversation."

Not waiting for a response, Rayna hung the phone up. She was not surprised by her tears. She felt the strong embrace of rejection again. She was too tired to fight its hold. It would win this night. With a heavy heart, she drifted off to sleep.

Chapter 11

She looked around at her surroundings in confusion. She couldn't see; the fog was heavy. She was on some type of path. A brisk wind caused the leaves to whirl around at her feet. She should have felt cold from the wind, but she felt nothing. She could hear the distant cry of a baby in distress. Concerned for the baby spurted her actions, she had to reach the baby. Swirling around in a circle, she began to panic. She struggled to find the direction of the baby's cry. Her feet had grown heavy; it felt like something was pulling her down. The baby was crying louder now. She forced her feet to move.

Finally, she was able to move freely, and the fog was beginning to clear. She found herself walking down a long and narrow corridor. She walked for what felt like hours. At last, standing before a door, she opened it and saw what appeared to be a nursery. There was a white crib with two stuffed pink elephants inside it. On the wall was a mural of a garden, next to it was a waterfall. The garden looked so lifelike. Awed, Rayna reached out to touch the mural.

Hearing a baby's cry again, she whirled around, her eyes resting on the crib by the window. She walked quickly to the crib. Swallowing hard, Rayna's heart lurched. She had thought the crib was empty at first. Not so. Inside the crib was a beautiful baby girl. Rayna picked the baby up and began to rock her in her arms. Cooing softly to the baby, she was awarded a gummy smile in response. Rayna's heart leaped in response.

This was her world. She was a wife and mother. Moreover, she was happy. In this world, everything was perfect. Rayna smiled in her sleep, as she cradled her baby in her arms. A solid figure stood behind her, wrapping his strong arms around her. The love in his eyes made her weak in the knees. He bent down to kiss the baby.

"You have made me a happy man," the familiar voice said.

Rayna sat straight up in bed. She remembered! She had met Eric at the office. She looked wildly around the room, half expecting Eric to be in there with her. It was a dream, but it felt so real. Her body began to shake with tears. The anguish came from the visceral of her being. It was the cry of the wounded. It was the cry of being a defected woman. The cry of never being able to give her heart to any man. Who would want half a woman? She could never have children. She accepted her shortcoming. However, it still hurt. Just when she thought she was over it, something always came up, reminding her that she was barren. She did not fault or blame Eric. He probably did her a favor in not pursuing a relationship with her.

Was it God's way of telling her she was destined to be alone? Paul in the Bible was alone. She cried harder. She did not want to be a Paul. She wanted to be an Esther. She wanted her King to find her, making her his Queen. She cried until she could cry no more. She cried until the stars and moon descended. Blessedly, sleep finally claimed her, giving her a brief reprieve from her pain. As she drifted off, she thought again of Eric. She could never give him what he wanted...a family.

* * *

It was time. This was the night. She could have sworn that she had never seen a dark night like this in all her years alive. Not a single star hung in the sky. There was no moon. The wind was still. The night seemed foreboding. She almost reneged on her promise of escape. She had to leave this very night. Her instincts told her this. No, the voice told her this. *You haven't much time, little one. Make haste now!*

The warning was the fuel to ignite her fire. Jamming her feet into her worn running shoes, she began to fling her meager possessions into her book bag. Pulling the rickety dresser drawer out from against the wall, she bent down and pulled up a piece of floorboard, and took out the money she'd hidden for emergency escapes. She looked at the faded documents also hidden, and tears sprang to her eyes as memories of old surfaced.

VANESSA RICHARDSON

Hurry, your time is almost up. Go out the back and remember, stay to the shadows. You must live this night. You must. The woman grabbed the documents, her bag, and ran to the window. Without thought, she leaped out the two-story window. The bulk she was carrying made landing awkward. Not allowing herself time to rest. She jumped to her feet and began to run, remembering, as always, to stick to the shadows.

The car came out of nowhere. It was a black sedan. Its windows tinted dark. She skirted to a halt. The car parked in front of her apartment building. Fear paralyzed her. Clutching her bag to her, she tried to control her breathing. The added weight was slowing her down. Her heart felt as though it was going to explode. She bent waist down, in an attempt to catch her breath. She rubbed her stomach, relieving the ache. Little white dots flashed behind her eyes, she was going to faint she realized. *Breathe!* She long since learned to listen to the voice. She called it her guide. The voice only spoke when she was in grave danger.

Three men exited the car. The darkness of the night obscured their features. Their steps were in unison, almost like a dance. One deviant stopped, while the other two continued into the building. Without warning, the deviant suddenly swung his head in her direction.

Gasping in shock, she instinctively flattened herself to the wall. Crouching on her knees, she began crawling further back into the alley. She could hear the stranger's slow prowl coming closer. Tears began to course down her face. She tried to crawl as fast as she could, without revealing her presence. She moaned as sharp shards of glass became embedded into her knees and hands. She crouched up against the wall, pulling the broken glass from her knees. It was her left hand she was most concerned with. The glass embedded there was three inches in diameter. She bit her lip, tasting blood, and pulled out the glass. Immediately, blood began to ooze. She retrieved a cloth from her bag. He was close.

Do not move. She pushed her damp hair from her face and waited. She made her body as small as she could. She felt the darkness then. He was close enough for her to smell him. His scent, like him, was unique. The woman was sure she would never forget his smell as long as she lived.

His shoes were black and immaculate. He was in front of her. The mounds of trash bags helped to obscure her presence from him. The stranger rested on his haunches, sharply inhaling. Her eyes widened when she saw her bloody rag a couple of meters from his feet. She held her breath, sweat was falling, but she dared not move. She felt something land heavily on her shoulder. It took brute strength for her not to cry out. The will to live made it tenable for her to not move.

"We have a ghost, boss. The house is empty," a voice stated.

The dark one rose up swinging, hitting the air in frustration. "It seems our target has escaped us again." He took out a black handkerchief and began to wipe his mouth. Saliva formed heavily in his mouth. For years he suffered from a saliva disorder. Whenever he spoke, saliva would spew forth.

At the sound of movement, both men turned, drawing their weapons. They slowly lowered them upon seeing a big gray alley cat. He knelt down again, wiping his shades with a dark handkerchief.

"The alley can't always keep you safe. Soon the kitty cat is going to be caught. She is running out of lives." The deviant stood and left the alley.

The woman collapsed against the wall and cried. She was trembling so hard, she could hear her teeth chattering, and her head was hitting the wall. A noise caused her to lift her head. A score of alley rats where everywhere. Shrieking, she stood clutching her precious bag, and began limping out of the alley.

The voice was silent again. That meant she was safe for now. The deviant was right; she was running out of time. She needed a plan and a place to lay low for a while. She must rest. She was so very tired. Only twenty-four years old, but she felt older.

VANESSA RICHARDSON

She remembered the woman from the Women's Shelter. She was her last resource. She hated to involve her, but there was no way around it. All her other options have been depleted. Besides, she was tired of the running. It was time. First, she must rest in preparation of what was to come. She prayed the woman at the center would not let her down.

Chapter 12

She always felt a sense of comfort when she entered the sanctuary. As usual, the church was packed, and the atmosphere was percolating with excitement and anticipation of Pastor Bryan Montgomery's installation as Assistant Pastor.

The Mother's Board was dressed in their usual garb of all white. Their big white hats were bobbing up and down, as they enthusiastically embraced the youths. Sheila sat next to a serene Rayna. This bothered her, as Rayna was always chipper and upbeat. When Sheila inquired what was wrong, Rayna just smiled and said she had a late night. Sheila was hurt and was not going to be put off that easily. The two had been through too much together. After service, they were going to have a sister-to-sister pow-wow.

Sheila was doing her best to appear calm, but it was a losing battle. Her nerves were frayed, and her insecurities were resurfacing. Looking at her best friend, she once again was struck by how beautiful she was. Rayna was not just esthetically beautiful, she was beautiful inside and out.

Today, Rayna wore a two-piece burgundy dress suit with a gold metallic sheen to it, enhancing her almond-shaped eyes. Her long wavy locks, which would normally be in a bun, were hanging gloriously free. Gold studs graced her ears, and around her slender neck was her ever-faithful gold cross.

Sheila glanced down at her own wardrobe and smiled. She had to admit that she looked good. It was taking some getting use to the new woman she was today, but she was getting there. She still had her moments. *However, I will deal with them*, she affirmed to herself.

"You know he's looking for wife number two, right?" came a syrupy voice from behind. Sheila wanted to turn around and see who the voice belonged to. She thought she recognized its owner, but wasn't certain.

VANESSA RICHARDSON

Another voice chimed in. "Sister Harper, you know I don't pay attention to the lapping lips of people. It's quite disgusting, and those who do, need to quickly get a life." The woman's voice had hardened.

"I mean it's utterly ridiculous. Sister Vance, the things I have been seeing would shock the Pope." She emphasized the word seeing. "It makes me want to run to the altar and repent for them." Sister Harper's voice grew louder. "Well, I'm just doing my Christian duty. After all, we are our brother's keeper. These women are drawing to him as buzzards to road kill. It's just pure shamefulness."

"And just who might these brazen ones be, Sister Harper?" Sister Vance asked.

"Now, now, Sister Vance, I cannot say any names, as that would be unchristian of me. Just pray for the young Montgomery men. Um hum, these new millennium Jezebels; going after married men too. Stolen water is temptation. These modern day women are nothing like the women of yesterday. We knew the value of our reputation. My, my, my, those handsome Montgomery boys are going to need all the prayers they can get," Sister Harper said.

Sheila's heart began to accelerate. Suddenly it felt as though everyone was looking at her. Looking around the beautiful church edifice, she noticed the scores of young beautiful women. All impeccably dressed, nails done, and skin glowing. She felt the old shy and lost Sheila wanting to resurface. She felt like leaving. However, she was tired of running, she had come a long way and refused to take two steps back.

If Mike wanted to play the pick-a-wife game, then he was certainly free to do so, only she was not going to be a participant of the game. Sheila opened her Bible forcefully, crossed her legs, and firmly resolved to put Mike out of her mind for good.

Rayna stared at Sheila in concern. She knew Sheila felt her stare, but she refused to acknowledge it. She kept her eyes trained on a passage in the Bible. Sighing, Rayna turned around, offering up a prayer for her friend. It was all up to Sheila; true happiness was at her door. If she wanted to be happy, she would have to make the right decision to do so. People are always going to find something bad to say about a person. They persecuted Jesus, and He was perfect.

"Sheila, I trust that you're big enough not to let trivial gossip ruin your chance at happiness with Mike." Sheila arched one perfectly sculpted brow, but said nothing.

Rayna knew that look all too well. There would be no getting through to her friend on this matter. Expelling a breath, Rayna offered up another prayer to the Lord. She had a feeling Mike was in for the fight of his life.

The silence was the first indicator of Mike's arrival. Sheila counted ten seconds of silence; then the resuming of the incessant chattering of single hopefuls vying for the attention of Pastor Montgomery's eligible son. The second indicator was the prickling of her skin. This happened whenever she was around Mike. What did that mean? Maybe she was allergic to him. That would be her luck.

"Hello ladies." Mike's eyes never wavered from Sheila's face. The smile that he wore slowly disappeared. He sensed all was not well on the home front.

Rayna offered her gustatory greeting, while Sheila only nodded. "Hey there, Mike. Good to see you," she said.

Mike bowed slightly at the waist. "Rayna, the pleasure, as always is mine."

Rayna nudged Sheila, and dramatically began fanning herself. "My, my, you see, Sheila, my dear friend, chivalry is not dead." Rayna liked Mike's old world style.

Other women may find it archaic and out of place, but to her it was enduring and refreshing. She knew Sheila appreciated it too; the slight smile she was sporting was evidence enough. Sheila murmured something under her voice. Standing Rayna excused herself, claiming the need for a ladies room break before service began. Sheila glared at her friend's retreating back.

Taking the seat Rayna vacated, Mike smiled in greeting. Sheila looked alarmed.

"That was not so subtle," Mike said smiling.

"Yeah, Rayna never was one to take the subtle approach. She is who she is, and that's what I love and admire about her. Although, right now, I feel the need to have a meeting in the ladies room with her," Sheila said.

She could again feel the force of hostile stares of the single hopefuls, and once again, felt like bolting from the sanctuary. She began to shift in her seat. Suddenly, the room seemed to shrink. She reached for one of the fans in the pocket of the church seat in front of her, and began to fan herself rapidly.

"Rayna does what she wants, when she wants. If she wants you to know something then you will know it. If she does not want you to know then you will not. She didn't get to be one of the best lawyers in Atlanta for nothing."

"No, not at all," was all Mike could think to say. He was confused. This was not the Sheila he'd taken to lunch a couple of days ago. That Sheila was carefree and warm. This Sheila was aloof and distant.

He mentally began to review their date, wondering what he had done wrong, and came up blank. He thought that their date had gone great. Maybe he was wrong. Wanting her all to himself that day, he drove them to the next county to eliminate interruption from the town people. They ate at a small intimate diner owned by a friend of his from college. The food and conversation was stellar.

With each passing moment, Mike felt himself being pulled into Sheila's life. He understood now that God had placed her in his life for such a time as this. He was certain that she was his gift from God. He would value it always. That moment, he offered up a prayer of thanksgiving to God. Vowing to be the man God wanted him to be.

Could it be possible for her to be anymore beautiful? She was stunning. He noticed a small beauty mark near her left eye. Had it always been there? Her wealth of dark hair fell to her shoulders. She wore little make up, she didn't need it as she had a natural beauty about her. Sheila was real. That was what he liked most about her, her ability to be real. That was a rare trait in this time and age.

Mike's cologne was playing havoc with Sheila's senses. She was losing this battle; it was too much too soon. A man like Mike did not date women like her.

"You see what I mean? Some women are so desperate. She has been to church quite regularly. It doesn't take Sherlock Holmes to figure out why. Umm, can we say Brother Michael?" Sister Harper stated bitterly.

"I do see your point now, Sister Harper," Sister Vance placated. "It's a shame the lengths some women will go to get a man. Lord, have mercy upon us all."

Sheila's stomach clenched at their barbs. It was suddenly becoming difficult to breathe. It seemed that everyone was looking and pointing fingers at her. Is that what people thought of her? That she was some vixen after the pastor's son?

Mike glanced sharply in her direction. "Sheila?" His voice held concern. She jumped up so quickly, she inadvertently hit Mike in the face with her purse.

"Oh, my goodness, I'm so sorry." Sheila cupped Mike's face, trying to assess her damage. He placed his hands on top of hers, their gaze locking. "Please excuse me, I have to go." She had to get out. She tried to remove her hand, but Mike refused to release it.

"Did you just see that? She assaulted the Pastor's son with her purse. Where are the ushers?" Sister Vance cried out.

Sister Harper gasped in outrage. "Really, some people have no respect for the house of God and now it seems His worshippers too."

"Where are the ushers when you need them?" Sister Vance looked around the sanctuary for an usher.

"It's the spirit of the Jezebel. It's running rampant," Sister Harper stated proudly.

It amazed Sheila how, in an instant, things could change from good to bad. Upon first arriving, she was awed by the beautiful church edifice, and was excited to establish a church home. Now it seemed like the walls were closing in on her. She did not belong. She would never belong.

Mike rubbed the spot where Sheila's purse made contact, but refused to let Sheila pass. He felt his anger surfacing, but he knew that church was a place of worshiping and praising. If a person could not find comfort in the house of God, then something was greatly amiss. He was not a violent person; however, the hurt in Sheila's eyes wanted him to hit something.

Slowly, he released Sheila's hand, and immediately felt the disconnection.

"It was an accident. Don't let bitter ranting of others do this to you. It's obvious they're lacking something or someone." Mike said with emphasis, and was pleased by the gasp of shock he received. "Please stay," he said.

"Well, I do believe he was talking about us, Sister Vance," Sister Harper said.

"I will agree with you, Sister Harper. I'm not going to sit here and be insulted for revealing Satan's plans. Come along, Sister Harper, I'm going to my sister's church. It's where we should have gone in first place. There they only take up one offering," Sister Vance said.

Sister Harper reached down, collecting her purse and worn Bible. "Well, that's fine with me. I'm tired of paying for a blessing anyways."

An usher came forth with a worried look on her face. Sister Vance, the taller of the two women, looked down her long nose at the usher.

"Well, it is about time you showed up," Sister Vance stated scathingly at the head usher. "There is a lot to be said about your timing, Sister Harvey. Would you like God to be late when you need Him?"

"Is there a problem here?" Sister Harvey asked. There was a steely command to the question. It was obvious that she took her ushering position seriously.

LOVE FOUND ME

Sister Vance merely shrugged, walking off, while Sister Harper motioned her head toward Sheila. "Therein lays the problem. Good luck with it," she said.

Mike smiled at the usher. He knew Sister Harvey; she used to baby-sit him and his brother. She was stern but fair. Right now, she gave him a look saying, *don't test me. What are you doing?*

Things were getting out of hand. Sheila just held her head down. Every manly instinct in him wanted to gather Sheila in his arms and comfort her, but he sensed she would balk from any comfort from him. He could not risk the rejection. Besides, this was not the time or place. Standing slowly, he reluctantly let her pass.

"Sheila?" Mike whispered. "People are going to talk, good or bad. They have nothing to do with you and me. You cannot keep running. If you want me to announce it to the church I will." He felt desperate. Somehow, he felt he was losing Sheila. He did not want that to happen.

"I cannot be the woman you want. The woman you need." Sheila's voice cracked. Great, now she was about to cry. "I'm sorry." She practically ran from the sanctuary, nearly plowing into Rayna.

"Whoa. What's going on?" a shocked Rayna demanded. She had never seen her best friend this distraught before. Sheila was sweating profusely, and was breathing too hard. Rayna led her over to one of the soft chairs in the church lobby. "Sheila, breathe slowly," she said.

"I'm sorry, Rayna. I just remembered I have some documents that I have to collect from my office." Sheila avoided Rayna's eyes. She prayed Rayna would for once let her have this moment.

Rayna looked from Sheila to the silently approaching Mike. Rayna shrugged.

"Okay then. I'll take copious notes from Pastor's sermon. Call me later, okay?" Rayna gently touched Sheila's shoulder in passing.

"Thanks. I will." Sheila smiled softly, grateful to have Rayna as a friend.

Rayna touched Mike's hands in encouragement. He was renewed by the support she was offering. He knew he was in a battle for his lady's heart. Something or someone had hurt her, and it was causing her to shut him out. He had to be careful with her. *God, show me what to do.*

"Sheila, can we go somewhere private to talk?" Mike stepped closer, placing a finger on her mouth, stifling her protest.

"Please, don't do this," Sheila pleaded.

Mike felt that if they were to talk she would give him...them a chance. He was now more certain than ever, that providence had drawn them together. He was being given another chance at happiness, and he was going to embrace it.

Sheila felt confused and scared at the same time. Mike's eyes were begging her to say yes, and she wanted to. She wanted to give this man anything he wanted, but she was afraid. How could someone like her possibly satisfy a man like Mike? She was way out of her league.

Sheila grabbed Mike's hand in support. "Mike, look, this is all wrong. All wrong. I don't want this."

Mike leaned forward. "Can we please go get a cup of coffee and just talk?" He was mentally coaxing her to agree with his request. "Please."

Sheila surrendered. Nodding her head, she smiled in acquiesce. Mike released the breath he wasn't aware of holding. Now the battle would begin and he was ready.

Chapter 13

Arriving fifteen minutes later at the Java Hut, Mike slid in the seat across from Sheila. He really wanted to sit next to her and hold her hands, but he knew she wasn't ready for such an open display of affection from him.

Mike and Sheila ordered cappuccinos and slices of blueberry cheesecake. Sheila needed all the comfort she could get for the conversation ahead of them. She sensed both of them needed this time of releasing and sharing together. She looked around at the small cafe shop, and was very much impressed by its ambiance. There was an old jukebox in the corner, which was playing soft classical music. On the walls were pictures of past and present celebrities. Mike waited as Sheila surveyed the restaurant. He was trying to picture it through her mind.

"This is a lovely place. Thanks for bringing me here," she said. Mike smiled, feeling like he was just given an award.

"This place is awesome. Every Sunday is poetry night. I have to tell you, there are some fierce poets gracing that stage. Sharon, the owner, is particular as to whom she lets perform here. Her motto is to feed the body and the soul. You're going to love their cheesecake." Lowering his voice, Mike leaned forward. "Don't tell anyone, because she thinks we don't know this. But my mother oftentimes bought two or three of their cheesecakes during the Christmas holidays. Every year we complimented her, and every year she states it wasn't her, but the master chef." Mike chuckled softly.

"For years I thought she was referencing God. Until one day, I came here and ordered the cheesecake. As I was eating it, I could have sworn I'd eaten here before, but that was impossible, because it was my first visit here."

Sheila leaned in close, eyes wide with anticipation. Mike liked that he had her full attention; he tempted to add on to the story to prolong the moment.

"Wanting to compliment the creator of such a fine creation, I requested to see the pastry chef. He came out wearing an apron that read 'Master Chef'. It was then that I put two and two together." Mike and Sheila laughed, it was an icebreaker.

Mike felt the change in the atmosphere. Looking up, he saw Sharon, the owner of the Java reach for the microphone. "I think we're about to hear some poetry," he said. Sheila followed Mike's direction to the stage.

"Ladies and gentlemen, you're in for a treat tonight. Our guest poet tonight is none other than Lady Happening."

Sheila's eyes widened and her mouth flew open at the introduction. Lady Happening was one of the most sought out poets in the world. She was a younger Maya Angelou. Mike knew he had done the right thing when Sheila reached out and squeezed his hand.

"Please give it up for Lady Happening." Instead of applause, the audience began snapping their fingers. Sheila and Mike immediately joined in.

"Thank you so much. I'm so delighted to be here amongst you tonight. I'm a huge fan of cheesecake, and was told if I wanted a slice of the best cheesecake in the world I should come here. I'm glad I did. I was also told that if I wanted to spread some love via poetry, I could. So, please allow me to share with you a piece I've written titled *The Unforgettable One*. Sheila sat straight up in her seat, anxious to hear the poet's words.

The Unforgettable One

Love found me
I was hidden from plain view.
Hidden from you.
I was lost. But love found me.
The battle for me was not easy.
I was once betrayed.
Beloved, hear the words of my heart.

LOVE FOUND ME

I want to embrace this new start.
I was afraid.
I was afraid that one day you would leave me.
Happiness had a way of teasing me.
True love was fleeting to me.
In the end, love found me.
Love has a way of making the world look colorful.
Before you, my world was dismal.
I was looking. Now I am seeing.
I looked at the sun and felt nothing.
I looked at the moon and felt nothing.
You accepted me. My flaws and all.
You didn't try to change me.
Your realness enhanced me. I thank God for you.
Your love has found me.
Past hurts and rejections.
From these things your love has set me free.
Now I know how to love and be loved.
My Mr. Right came into my life.
And along with him came great delight.
For my love, he didn't have to fight.
Everything in my life was all right.
I ran to him and not from him.
We will grow together.
Over comes the stormy weather.
I am so blessed.
Love found me.

Sheila sat transfixed by the words flowing from the young poet's mouth. She was speaking the words that were in Sheila's heart. Mike simply watched Sheila. He couldn't help it; there was an innocent beauty about her. They had dimmed the lights, and Sheila's skin seemed to glow under the fluorescent lights.

"Sheila, I can understand your fears. This...what we're feeling is scary for me. But I'd rather deal with the fear than run from it. I know better than anyone that running doesn't solve anything. You have to confront it. Don't run from this, Sheila...from us." Her eyes grew wide with shock. Reaching across the table, Mike captured her hands in his.

Sheila was stunned at Mike's confession. The fact that he wanted to be with her was frightening. She didn't know what to do with a man like Mike. He was intelligent, confident and secure. She was his polar opposite. It couldn't work; she would be his Achilles heels.

Looking into Mike's eyes, she could see he wanted to tell her something. Squeezing his hands in support, she prompted him to continue. Mike looked out the window. Sheila could see that he was in a different place. He began to talk, his voice sounding distant.

"I was married once, and was deeply in love. We knew each other since high school. When I first saw her, I knew that she would one day be my wife." Mike laughed softly. "I was bold enough to tell her such."

Sheila wasn't quite sure what she was feeling. Hearing Mike confess his love of another woman was unsettling, but this was not about her, it was about him. Sheila was ashamed of herself for being selfish. Leaning in closer, she squeezed Mike's hand for encouragement. He smiled, accepting her comfort.

For a moment, she thought Mike wouldn't continue with his story. His head was bowed, yet he said nothing. Sheila stilled, afraid if she moved he would stop his story. She knew he had to see this out. She really looked at him with the heart of a woman in love with a man. She saw past the exterior, seeing for the first time the true man that Mike was. He was loving, self-sacrificing and trustworthy. Right now he needed her.

"She was a genius. Her IQ scores where very high. She was generous-- almost to a fault." Mike pinched the bridge of his nose. "I can count the times she completed her supposedly friends homework because they had suddenly become sick. After we graduated from high school, we both attended Howard University. She majored in Psychology, I in Law. We got married immediately after college. She got a job as a high school counselor. I went on to Law School. Two years later, we discovered we were going to be parents." Mike finally looked into Sheila's eyes. The hurt in his eyes was so evident; it made her want to cry.

"I wanted to tell the world I was going to be a daddy. I wanted to celebrate the occasion." Mike's voice trailed off. He was silent for so long, Sheila was afraid he would not continue. He released her hand, and she immediately missed his touch. Sipping from his cup, Mike once again claimed Sheila's hand. She smiled. She placed her right hand on his, gently squeezing. Mike smiled and nodded his head.

"Thank you for sharing that much with me, Mike. If this is too painful for you, please don't continue, I understand. All things take time." Sheila smiled at her man.

Yes, she accepted that Mike was her man. She was tired of the running. If God saw fit to bring a wonderful man like Mike into her life, then who was she to kick against the grain. Stunned, Mike set straight up in his seat. He noticed the change in Sheila immediately. This phenomenon was unexplainable, and how was it possible to be so in tune to someone you have recently met. Yet, he and Sheila were living proof that it could happen. It was divine connection, he was sure of it.

Two butterflies dancing outside the restaurant caught Mike's attention. The butterflies were dancing wildly, their bright colors reminding him of the rainbow. He recalled that the rainbow in the Bible was symbolic for the promise of God. Could God grant him another chance at happiness? If he were without hesitation, he would take it, but first, he had to release the past.

"Leaving the restaurant, we encountered a severe thunderstorm," Mike said, continuing with his story. His voice was so soft Sheila had to lean forward to hear him. "I have never experienced a storm like that in my days. It came out of nowhere. The wind tossed our car around like it was a rag doll. The rain wouldn't stop. I ran over something, causing us to have a flat tire. I got out to change the flat tire. Suddenly this car came out of nowhere. It's assumed that the driver must have been drunk or something." Sheila wondered about Mike's last statement. "The driver rammed into us. I was tossed several feet into the air, landing in a nearby ditch. My wife never made it out of the vehicle; it exploded, killing both her and my unborn child." Looking out the window again, Mike swallowed hard. "They didn't have a chance; gone too soon. We're still looking for the perpetrator. It's a hard case to solve, because I couldn't see anything that night."

He looked into Sheila's eyes, his heart warming at what he saw. She was crying. Her grip on his hands was painful, but he did not want her to let him go.

"Please, don't leave me, Sheila. I never thought that I would be able to open my heart to anyone again. I do not know why God chose to give me another chance, but I'm willing to take it."

"Do you really feel God had something to do with this, Mike? And are you sure this is what you want?" Sheila asked. She was aware that Mike had not spoken his wife's name. Was he really ready to move on? Would she have to contend with the ghosts from his past?

"There is no doubt in my heart about that. I was broken. No one could help me in my brokenness. I remember going to God and just being real with Him because I didn't understand why. Why my wife? Why my unborn child? Why I didn't die?" Sheila gasped and tightened her hold on Mike's hand. "I don't think that way anymore. It was a process. However, I'm wiser now. Different-- but wiser."

"Mike, you've been through Hell and back. I'm so sorry for the losses you have suffered." Sheila moved closer and softly cupped Mike's face. He immediately leaned in, accepting her comfort. "I'm scared, and tired of the running. If you are brave enough to stand in acceptance of God's will, then so shall I. I want to see where this," Sheila waved a hand in their direction, "is going to take us. I hope it's into our future together, Mike, because I have never felt like this towards anyone, especially in such a short time." She leaned in closer to Mike. "Is this kind of thing possible, Mike?"

LOVE FOUND ME

Mike's heart soared at her announcement. God was giving him another chance at happiness. He looked at the beautiful woman across from him. She was his gift, his treasure. He would prove to her his love and devotion. He knew now, as he knew with Marie, that he was looking into the eyes of his wife. He immediately bowed his head and thanked God.

"Sheila, fear is the last thing I want you to feel towards me. I cannot explain this phenomenon between you and me. What I'm sure about is I want...need you in my life, Sheila." It was a plea, but he didn't care. He was in a battle for the love of his life, and he was going to use everything in him to win.

Sheila smiled at Mike's words, evaporating any fear she had. Mike returned her smile and her heart soared. Maybe everything was going to be all right. Perhaps it was her time at true happiness, to love and to be loved.

Chapter 14

The dark one stared out the window. Nothing mattered except finding her. Twelve elusive years his prey was able to avoid capture. She was the one. He could feel it. The set time for Zion was now. The tribe was growing restless. The tribe he could handle. When his time to reign takes place, he would deal with them sufficiently.

It was the Triune he was worried about. They were becoming impatient. The people were ready for their leader to come and lead them as the prophecy spoke of. He reminisced over the last meeting before the Triune.

He was being led down a dark corridor by two men garbed in black robes; the hood they wore masking their identities. It didn't matter to the man. He was focused on what to say to counsel. One of the masked men keyed in some numbers on a number pad on the wall. The door opened, and a smell so foul emanated, which didn't bother either man. The men were used to the smell, so they embraced it. It was the smell of rotting fish. The two men stepped back, and he continued in alone. No one entered unless invited. That was a major rule never to be ignored. He entered but stayed close to the door. In the center of the floor was a diagram of a five-pointed star with interwoven sides.

"Come forth." The man entered the darkened room, standing directly on the diagram. Three figures were clad in dark red robes. They were sitting in high throne chairs perched high on a dais.

"Have you found the one?" Dimitri asked. He was the leader of the three.

"The people grow restless," Stone said. He was second in command.

"I have indeed found the one. I will take my rightful place and lead our people into greatness as the prophecy spoke of," the dark one announced. The Triune looked around.

"Where is she?" Dimitri demanded.

"Why are you alone?" questioned Stone.

"He rambles on as the rest of them did. I say we be rid of him for wasting our time." This came from Loren. Of the three, he was the most evil. He allowed action to dictate his decisions; rather than ration. He took pleasure in making people suffer, the screams of pain and agony was like a high for him.

Another place and time, he would have loved to connect with him. He was not afraid of Triune. He thought them weak, nuisances really. He was waiting for his time of reign. When he became ruler, he would eradicate these three weaklings. He would anoint a stronger governing body.

Loren's eyes widened. He smiled sinisterly, revealing broken yellow teeth. The man cringed inwardly. He forgot to guard his emotions around Loren. Of the three, he was good at discerning emotions and feelings. It was almost as if he reads minds. He lowered his eyes.

"I ask that counsel grant me permission to speak." He bowed slowly on one knee, remembering to keep his head lowered. The three glanced at each other simultaneously, nodding their heads.

"Permission granted." Dimitri leaned forward, waiting.

Rising to his feet, he raised both hands in surrender position and nodded. "She continues to evade me. She is heavy with child and is now slow with movement. I know where she is, and this time she won't escape. The next time I come before counsel, it will be with her. And I will be anointed as the new leader of Zion."

Again, the Triune looked at each other and nodded. These looks always angered him. It made him feel as if he was being mocked, as if they knew something he didn't. He slowly lowered his hands to his side.

Again, it was Dimitri who spoke. "Your words are the same of yesteryear. Could it be that you have failed and that you are not the chosen one to lead Zion?"

Stone nodded. "I concur. You're a waste of time and breath. I grow weary of this cat and mouse game you're caught up in. Time is something we don't have!" The loudness of his words vibrated off the walls. His eyes were bloodshot, as if he hadn't slept in days. Around his mouth was something brown and crusty looking. He swiped out his tongue, wiping it away. "Tell us, how a slip of a girl manages to evade you this long? Certainly, this is a testament of your leadership skills." He spared a look at the other two leaders, their stares remained fixed on the man in front of them. "Yes, perhaps you are not the one. Zion is in need of a leader who knows how to get the job done. He utilizes every weapon at his disposal; he will create them when there is none. He is able to see before anyone else does."

The man hastily bowed down again on one knee. "I am that man. Zion will be resurrected under me, and we will grow and flourish. Right now, I have servants in high positions, in local and head governments. They are waiting and ready for me...for Zion!"

The three looked at each other again. Their gazes locked longer than he would have liked. He held his breath and waited. If they denied him, he vowed to kill them all right there on the spot. He slowly slid his hand inside his jacket, feeling the gun nestled where he left it. He would go down fighting.

"Very well then, the Triune has granted you permission, for the final time to continue with your quest." Dimitri leaned his head to the side, smiling sinisterly-- as if he held a secret. "Go and bring her back and let the prophecy be fulfilled."

Loren laughed mirthlessly. "And know this, damned one." The man's brow lifted at being called damned. If anyone was damned it was these three. He remained silent. "If you don't bring her back," he paused, leaning forth, "the next time you come before counsel it will be your last time. I will personally clean you up, and will enjoy doing so."

"You are dismissed." Stone waved a hand impatiently. He was tempted to use his weapon right then and there. A knock at the door interrupted his rumination.   "Enter," he said.

LOVE FOUND ME

"Sir, we think we have found her."

"I do not need for you to think, Roscoe. I need for you to know. I'm growing tired of this cat and mouse game. Time is wasting and I want her now!" The dark one's voice rose higher. As he talked, spit was flying everywhere, and his eyes were bloodshot red. The man's Adam's apple bobbed up and down with fright.

"Yes, sir, we are certain that we have found her next location. We will acquire her, sir," Roscoe said. Backing slowly out of the room, he bowed repeatedly.

Taking a worn photo of a young girl with sad brown eyes from his pocket, the dark one smiled. "You will soon be mine, little one." Lifting the photo to his nose, he inhaled deeply then began to lick the photo repeatedly. "Soon my sweet, real soon we will be reunited."

Chapter 15

It was the third Sunday, which meant the youths would be in charge of the morning service. Mike and Sheila arrived twenty minutes earlier than normal, as third Sundays were always packed. Again, Sheila could not get over the grandeur of the newly built church. It truly was breathtaking. The ceiling chandeliers sparkled like diamonds. She wanted to reach out and touch one. It was not the church beauty itself that affected her the most; it was the authentic love from within the church. The church members were so friendly and attentive.

Sheila was shocked that the ushers even remembered her name. At first, she thought maybe it was because of Mike, but immediately dismissed that notion. This was a true church family, and they authentically loved each other. Every Sunday they announced their sick list and up and coming birthdays. That right there required time. Yet they did it.

"I'm excited about the sermon my brother is going to preach today. He has a way with the young people. Our youth membership has increased a great deal since his arrival. No offense to Pop," Mike said, as they entered the church.

"Praise the Lord, Sister Sheila. It's good to see you this fine Sunday." An usher smiled in greeting.

"Sister Sheila, you looking good, baby." Mother Hattie broke through the throng of people, and wrapped Sheila in a fierce hug. Sheila hugged her back, almost crying as she remembered her nana, who had long since gone on to be with the Lord.

"Now listen to me, baby, don't you stay away too long. As often as you assemble yourself with us, you gain strength. Isn't that right, Mothers?" Mother Hattie said.

Another mother of the church also dressed in white, sandwiched Sheila's hands between hers. "That's right, little angel of the field. You make sure to assemble yourself amongst us frequently, and you will gain strength. We are sho' nuff Mothers of Zion, and we can get a prayer through when no one else can."

"That's right, little rutabaga. We have watched night services in our hearts. We got us Duracell hearts and minds. We keep going when no one else can. Let me show you the scars on my knees where I stay on 'em." This was from the third mother, who also wore white.

"Mother Grace, this baby doesn't need to see any scars this fine Sunday. She needs to see only good stuff." Mother Hattie did something Sheila was not expecting. She leaned in close to Sheila, and whispered, "Don't try to figure things out so much, baby, ya hear? God has seen your tears and He knows." She continued to pet Sheila's hand softly. "He knows." Mother Hattie began to buck, and for a moment, Sheila thought she was going to fall out. Ushers ran to her, but Mother Hattie only shrugged them away. Speaking in a foreign language, the other mothers soon followed.

"Use her Lord!" the Mothers chanted. "The light is all about you, Mother Hattie!"

Still holding Sheila's hand, Mother Hattie suddenly stilled. "Don't you fret about that situation; God is at work in your life. Trust God. Let go and let God. You keep the faith, hear baby. God is gonna come and see about you." With that, Mother Hattie and her entourage walked away, uttering in their secret tongues.

Mike, who was smart enough to keep his silence when it came to the fierce mothers, only smiled at Sheila.

"What was that all about, Mike?" Sheila asked.

He gazed down into Sheila's beautiful brown eyes, desperately wanting to hug her in comfort, but knew that would cause tongues to wag.

"I don't know, but whatever she said, believe her. Those ladies may be a little eccentric, but they are real for Jesus. Come on, let's go to our seats." Sheila allowed Mike to escort her to their seats, all the while pondering Mother Hattie's words in her heart.

The youth choir was something to behold. Sheila had no words for their performance. She didn't think at thirty years of age, she would feel so old and so out of sync with the latest youthful happenings. Her foster parents often took her to services. When she was in church, she had to sit and behave, and the song selection was mild and soul stirring. One look from her foster mama was all it took to still her fidgeting. All those things were key factors in her discontinuing going to church.

Today, the youth were moving to music, that years ago would not have been accepted. They were dressed in private school attire, and the lead singer had long dreads flowing down his back. He gave a soul stirring performance that left the congregation with mix reactions. The youth felt the spirit; the more seasoned looked confused as they offered their support.

"Let the Lord use you, baby." And some, "God works in unusual ways." And some, "We may not understand, but God does."

The youth choir finally settled down. Pastor Montgomery graced the podium. Sheila was excited; this would be her first time hearing the older Montgomery expound the written Word.

"Grace and blessings to you all. I'm delighted to be standing here today with a Rhema word for you. As you know, I have been on a spiritual shut-in for a couple of days. As your leader and Pastor, this is oftentimes necessary. I have been given an assignment. Turn with me to the book of Chronicles, Chapter 20."

Pastor Montgomery read the passage with such emotion; Sheila could actually see the characters in her mind. King Jehoshaphat was given the report that a multitude of his enemies from neighboring kingdoms wanted to destroy him. She could see how King Jehoshaphat would be fearful in the face of such adversity. She was awed of the battle technique he issued. His executive decision was to command the people of Judah to fast, denying them-selves food and prayed for victory.

"Beloved, some things you don't have to fight for. You should be like the palm tree, and just lean with it. King Jehoshaphat got past the fear and praised in advance. You have to see yourselves past the hurt, past the rejections. Then the melody that

God has placed in your hearts shall soar, becoming infectious. Your friends and family too shall join in your song of praise."

Mike reached for Sheila's hand and squeezed. She smiled, returning the squeeze.

"Mike," she whispered his name softly. She held his gaze. Mike understood her silent message. Smiling, he nodded. They were able to get past their fears and past struggles. Their union became their song of beginnings. Their song of happiness was infecting the ones around them.

Mike saw his brother smiling, and gave a small salute. Rayna was smiling, her eyes glittering with tears. She softly dabbed at her eyes. His mother winked, returning her gaze to his father. His father smiled.

"This song that God has placed in our hearts, keep it, let no one take it from you. It's yours, and the world can't take it away," Pastor Montgomery said.

Mike silently agreed with his father. God, in His infinite way, granted him a second chance at love. He vowed to do everything in his power to keep them together.

Chapter 16

Mike grunted loudly as he landed hard. He didn't want to move, every muscle in his body pleaded for him to stay down. It was for the third time that afternoon he found himself looking up at the sky. He loved his twin dearly, but at that moment, he was sorely tempted to strangle him. He couldn't do that, of course, without dividing his beloved family.

His parents would be upset with him, and would probably disown him. His sister-in-law, Valerie, would probably never speak to him again, and he'd hate for his niece and nephew to grow up without a father.

A shadow fell over him. A laughing Bryan extended his hand. A prideful wounded Mike grudgingly accepted his brother's help. Bryan was shaking his head, his lips perched.

"You're slacking, little brother. You've gotten lazy, not to mention a bit overweight." Bryan hit Mike on his flat stomach.

Mike didn't say a word; he continued bouncing the ball, feigning left and right. It's like Bryan knew every move he was going to make. Mike bounced the ball between his legs, turning around Bryan, he ran toward the goal. Mike was confident he was going to make the goal this time. He smiled in victory. Just when he was going for the slam-dunk, he heard his brother's warrior cry. Not good. Then *Swoosh!* The ball was knocked from his hand. Bryan reclaimed the ball, and immediately Mike went on the offense. Turning, he followed his brother, trying to steal the ball back. If Bryan made the shot, the game would be over. Mike swiped at the ball, but Bryan turned left and right, still dribbling the ball.

Mike couldn't help but to secretly admire his brother's skills on the court. He had game. Mike tried to regain possession of the ball, but it was too late, Bryan did a Kobe Bryant move, slamming the ball in the basket, defeating Mike 18-26. How humiliating. Mike wanted to slam his brother into the basket.

Bryan came up to him, not attempting to hide the smile forming. Mike decided he was going to be big about the situation. If his brother wanted to gloat like some adolescent, then he was more than welcome to do so.

"Good game, old man." Mike extended his hand to Bryan.

Bryan grabbed Mike in a big bear hug, rubbing his head roughly. Mike, irritated, pushed him away.

"Could have been better if your head was in the game," Bryan said.

"Good game, boys. Come and rest yourselves for a spell," their father called from his seat by the swimming pool.

Their parents were barbecuing today. The table was already set with his mother's family heirloom dinner sets. At the center of the table was a freshly made floral arrangement from his mother's flower garden. Mike couldn't help but admire the ambience produced by his sister-in-law and mother. *It looked like it could be featured in one of the Home Magazines women like to read,* he thought.

Bryan's wife and kids were in the kitchen with Mrs. Montgomery, helping to prepare lunch. After retrieving bottled waters from the cooler, Mike and Bryan joined their father by the pool. Pop had on a Bahamian shirt with some khaki shorts. On his feet was a pair of flip-flops. He looked like a tourist. As Mr. Montgomery watched his boys approaching, he felt great pride. He and his wife had always known they would have kids. When they were informed they were going to have twins, they were both surprised and deliriously happy. Although they looked alike, their personalities were different. Bryan was always the spokesman of the two. He was good with words. Mike was more action than words.

"You got creamed out there, Tabby. I thought you were going to bring your A game. That was like watching Kobe Bryant playing against your mother." Mike smiled at the nickname given to him by his pop. Pop peered at his boys from under his reading glasses. "And if you boys tell your mother I said that, you're both disowned permanently." Mike and Bryan laughed. "Son, it's been awhile, so don't worry about it. Just shake the cobwebs off and get back out there. You'll do better next time."

"Thanks Pops." Mike took a swig from his bottled water.

Pop raised his glass to Bryan. "You did well out there, Bo." Bryan nodded, acknowledging his nickname given to him by their father.

Bryan smiled broadly, saluting their pop with his bottled water. He suddenly sobered. "Thanks Pop." Shaking his head, he sighed loudly. "But like they say, if you don't use it, you'll lose it."

"Give it a rest, Bryan," Mike warned softly.

Bryan's eyes widened in mock innocence. He looked at their father in question, whose eyebrows went up. Pop hid a smile behind his beverage.

Sipping from his drink, their father faced Mike, and asked, "So, Mike, when your lady friend is coming?"

Mike warmed to the change of topic. "Saturdays are Sheila's busiest days. She plays catch up on her errands. I told her we would be dining at 6 o'clock." He looked at his watch; it was 4:30 pm. He had enough time to take a shower and run to the local florist to purchase some roses before Sheila arrived. He was both excited and nervous. Today, he was going to officially introduce Sheila to his family as his lady. He wanted to announce her as his wife, because there was no doubt in his mind that she was his wife. But he knew Sheila wasn't ready to hear that yet.

"I think it's a wonderful thing Sheila is doing. Her being a women's health advocate is awesome. Not everyone can handle that type of responsibility, and be affective at it," Bryan acknowledged.

Mike looked up but said nothing. He was feeling a bit guilty. He too admired Sheila for her dedication in helping those women out, but at the same time, he feared for her safety. She had shared with him some of the dangers she encountered due to her job selection.

LOVE FOUND ME

One day, they were sitting in the park feeding the squirrels, and Mike wanted to know more about her job. Sheila was hesitant at first. Shrugging gently, she confided in him the pros and cons of her job. She derived joy in helping the women build new lives. That same joy could easily turn to fear.

One time, an angry boyfriend of one her clients attacked her in her own office. Then there was the time when an irate husband smashed her car windows out. Sheila also confessed to him about the weird vibes she had surrounding her new client. Mike felt it was too much. He was becoming a maniac; her well being was hit top priority. For his peace of mind, he began a pattern of calling her at least three times a day, making sure she was all right. Sheila thought it was enduring.

Pop reclined back in his seat, slowly sipping his raspberry lemonade. Mike wasn't fooled by his casualness. Pop missed nothing. He was never one to rush into conversations. He allowed words to settle in, weighing them and then responding.

"I am certain job like that must come with quite a few hazards." He waved his hand. "I mean, you boys know how I counsel people from all walks of life. I've heard just about every problem there is." His voice dropped an octave, as if he were remembering past conversations. "One thing I know, you can't help a person unless they want to be helped."

Placing his beverage on the table, Mike stood and began pacing back and forth. He pinched the bridge of his nose, turned and he faced his father.

"Pop, I'm concerned about Sheila. I know she loves her job, but I don't think I can stand knowing everyday that her life is at risk."

The three men exchanged looks of understanding. The Montgomery men were very protective of their women. They took their roles as protector and provider seriously, almost to a fault. It wasn't that they were arrogant. It was an inherited trait the men had; that seemed to pass on from generation to generation. The women in their lives soon recognized this, and learned to accept this part of their man. Mike knew that Sheila would one day accept his protective side, but he didn't want her to change who she was in order to do so. Her job was a part of whom she was, and to ask her to give it up for his peace of mind just didn't sit well with him. He sighed heavily, and reclaimed his vacant seat. Bryan nodded.

"Well, have you talked to Sheila about this?" Bryan asked.

"I wanted to, but it seems like there is never the right time. Man, when she talks about her job, her eyes light up. It's like she is on some mission to save the world."

"Ah, mission impossible. Some people don't want to be saved." Bryan glanced at his father.

"Talk to her, son. You can't go into a relationship with fear and doubts. It can grow into something else...like distrust." Mr. Montgomery's brown eyes held concern. Placing his glass on the table, he leaned in close. "Tabby, make sure you've dealt with the past. Don't bring old fear into your new beginning." He paused, letting his words sink in. Mike nodded. "You owe it both to Sheila and yourself to be completely honest. Live in love and happiness, son, not fear."

Mike's face screwed up. "Pop, I just got her to agree to do the art exhibit; that was like pulling teeth. To ask her to change her occupation because of my fears..." He shrugged one broad shoulder, his voice trailing off.

"It will work itself out, son. Give it time," his father said.

Mike prayed that his father was right. How can he ask Sheila to give up something she loved doing just so he could feel at ease. Did she love him enough to do so? Mike didn't want to think about that just yet. Forcing the issue out of his mind for the time being, he concentrated on his family.

LOVE FOUND ME

Chapter 17

Sheila thought that she would be nervous. She was pleasantly surprised by how easily she was able to flow with the Montgomery's. Mike was trying so hard to make her feel welcome. He kept darting glances in her direction, asking her if she was all right. He was attentive and considerate. She fell a little deeper in love with him.

"Mike, would you leave that poor girl alone. You act as though she's in a lion's den. We aren't going to eat her," Mama chastised gently, her eyes wide with laughter.

Bryan was glad for the opening. "Actually we can get pretty rowdy around here. Mike is usually the ringleader. I want to share with you some stories of us growing up. Boy, did we give people something to talk about." He winked at Mike.

"I don't think Sheila would be interested in some old stories from the past," Mike said in warning.

"Of course I would, Mike," Sheila interrupted. Smiling, she reached out and patted his hand gently. "I would love to hear about your escapades growing up. Why, your being a twin and all, I'll bet there are some interesting stories to hear."

Mike set up straight, his gaze wary all at once. He had done some pretty outlandish things in his past. Some things he didn't think he wanted to share, not even with Sheila, it was too embarrassing. He had the prescience not to strangle his beloved twin at that moment. He'd wait until later. Bryan smiled at him. He turned and kissed his wife on the cheek, and she briefly rested her head on his shoulder. Mike's irritation vanished at their affectionate display of love for each other.

"Sheila, I've been meaning to compliment you on your outfit. The color is becoming on you," Bryan's wife complimented.

Sheila couldn't get over how closely Valerie resembled Michelle Obama. Her skin was a dark chocolate, and her dark thick hair hung loosely to her shoulder. She was wearing a green shirt that showed off toned arms, and a knee length skirt, complimenting her well defined legs.

"Thank you, Valerie. Purple is my favorite color. You're looking fierce yourself," Sheila said.

"We have got to get together and go shopping. I know the best places," Valerie said.

Sheila's heart dropped. She would never be able to afford one of Valerie's shopping sprees. Sheila was subtly inspecting her. Valerie oozed sophistication, even in a shirt and skirt.

"Mama Clara and I are a part of several nonprofit organizations. It can get pretty heavy dealing with all those red tapes and deep pockets. We call them 'Le résistant', don't we, Mama?" Valerie said.

Mama silently nodded, but murmured, "I'd like to call them something else, but it would be out of my character." Her comment caused a wave of laughter throughout the group.

Valerie met Sheila's eyes, continuing her speech. "So, Sheila, juxtapose that with family, work, and other obligations, it can burn a woman out. So, I set aside me some 'me' time."

Bryan tapped his glass with his fork, as if making an important announcement. "Let me just say; I love when my honey takes her 'me time', it benefits me also. 'Our time' is even sweeter. I don't know how it's possible, but she manages to return even more gorgeous."

Mike groaned. Pop continued to eat his food; murmuring something about sleep making you look and feel young. Mama was sporting a wide smile. She allowed her gaze to rest briefly on Mike and Sheila. Sheila swallowed hard. Mike suddenly became fascinated with his food.

"Awe. Thank you, sweetie." Valerie kissed Bryan softly on the cheek.

Bryan picked up his fork and knife, cutting happily into his baked chicken, all the while smiling like he'd just won the lottery.

Sheila was touched by their genuine display of love. She was never one to display public emotion, but she suddenly had a craving for that type of relationship. She found herself wanting to hold hands with Mike. He had some crumbs on the side of his mouth, which she wanted to reach out and remove. She looked at his broad shoulders. She wanted to rest her head on them.

Sheila took a bite out of her chicken, no longer tasting it. She wasn't naïve to believe all relationships were perfect. There would be ups and downs. Those things could only enhance their relationship, allowing them to get to know each other in good and the bad. She watched as Valerie wiped Bryan's mouth. She prayed that she and Mike would have that too.

From her peripheral side view, she could see Mike watching her. Was he too thinking the same thing? Turning, she met his gaze. He smiled, and she knew that he was. His smiled sent a zing through her system. She felt like she was free falling.

"Me time?" Sheila asked.

Valerie said excitedly, "This is when I take a couple days off, a sabbatical. One day doesn't cut it, for me, my friend. I just pamper me. Sometimes Mama Montgomery joins me. We have the most fun. The things we do are healthy mentally and physically. We get facials, pedicures, and incorporating some exercising into the mix."

Mama put down her knife and fork, clapping her hands together in delight. "It is all just wonderful Sheila. I agree; you should join us, dear."

Valerie smiled, nodding her head vigorously in agreement. Her eyes widening, she turned to Sheila. "Sheila, our next meeting is next week, oh, please won't you join us?"

Sheila swallowed nervously. She'd never been to a spa in her life. The closest she came to it was the local gym, which was presently having problems with its electrical system, causing the water to accelerate above normal heating temperature. She wouldn't know how to act; she'd make an idiot out of herself.

"I don't know, the center is quite busy and..." Sheila began to make her excuses.

Mrs. Montgomery waved off her flimsy excuse. "That center will be right there when you get back. Now, I won't take no for an answer. Once you join in our 'me time', you're going to thank me." Mrs. Montgomery leaned in close, as if she was about to reveal a hidden secret. "On our last day, we hold a 'we' attend service. It's for women only. We meet and just talk. Besides, it's my turn to treat." Mama picked up her knife and fork again, cutting gustily into a chicken leg, as if the matter was solved.

"Sheila, as a women's advocate director, you are going to love this group. These women are achievers and over comers. This wasn't always the case; there was a process to it." Valerie paused as if in thought. "In the beginning they are withdrawn and not trusting. We don't rush the process. We take our time finding out the root causes of their hurt, and then deal with it. I love our group's name...Women With Power." Valerie's intense eyes darted to Sheila's. "It's sad when a woman doesn't know her own power. Hurt and rejection can do that."

Sheila felt like Valerie was trying to tell her something.

"Women with Power: Our mission is to restore and establish, with the end results making us empowered." Sheila's eyes darted between Valerie and Mama Montgomery. Her excitement growing, she soon found she wanted to join in their 'me time'.

* * *

What a wonderful week it had been. She did something she had never done before. She took a week's vacation from her job. She accepted Mrs. Montgomery and Valerie up on their offer and joined in their 'me time'. Mama Montgomery wouldn't allow her to pay for anything, insisting that it was her treat. The truth was each Montgomery man was sponsoring their little getaway.

It was their last day at Hilton Head Island, South Carolina. Their week's itinerary consisted of the best spa treatment, facials, walks on the beach, and boat rides. The name fit...Women With Power.

LOVE FOUND ME

Sheila looked around at the array of women, hailing from all walks of life, and immediately felt a sense of belonging. The feeling brought tears to her eyes. She had invited Rayna to come along, but the case she was working on prevented her from coming.

Having met all the ladies during their week stay, Sheila felt she knew the ladies all her life. They all had commonness...overcoming adversities. She thought she had heard all there was when it came to women struggles, but these ladies had proven her wrong.

The ladies had assembled themselves in the backyard by a huge swimming pool shaped like a claw. There was a huge circular table and seven chairs. Sheila was seated in between Valerie and Mrs. Montgomery. She noticed on the table in front of each chair was a journal and a pen.

A beautiful full-figured woman stood tapping her glass of lemonade. Mrs. Forester, their hostess and owner of the mansion stood regally. Her cinnamon skin glowing, and a smile gracing her face. Her eyes expertly roamed across the sea of faces. Mrs. Forester and her husband were self-made millionaires. The Foresters' were products of humble beginnings. Mr. Forester invented one of the best creations known to woman...Fitted Ones, which was a mixture between a brassier and girdle. The product was slim trimming and less constrictive.

Mrs. Forester had watched her mother get attacked and killed when she was eight years old, the tragedy scarring her for life. She became reclusive, escaping in her studies. She had a Ph.D. in Women Studies, and teaches at the local community college. Mr. Forester, who was going through a painful divorce, knew she was the one when he first saw her at the grocery store. She had been concentrating on which milk brand to choose. He thought it was enduring. It was a battle winning her over, a battle well worth it. Now, thirty-eight years later, the couple was still madly in love with each other. Love has a way of finding you at the right time.

VANESSA RICHARDSON

"Ladies, as you can see," she smiled warmly at Sheila, "we have a visitor amongst us. She is the guest of our dear Clara Montgomery and Valerie Montgomery. Sheila Lawson."

Sheila acknowledged the many welcomed smiles. She wasn't accustomed to being the recipient of so many stares.

Mrs. Forester continued with her introduction. "Sheila works at The Mending Heart. She is an advocate for domestically abused women." This garnered several praises from the group. "We are on Chapter 5 in our pages of life." The women simultaneously opened their journals. "Natasha, I do believe it's your turn to share with us your story. Where are you on your pages of life?"

Natasha smiled. She was a petite woman with cinnamon colored skin. Her hair was short and curly, her eyes were light brown. They were shinning brightly. "I'm so happy to share my story with you. I open up with the word forgiveness."

At once, all the ladies began to write in their journals. Mrs. Montgomery nodded at Sheila, prompting her to follow suit. Natasha looked around the table, pausing, taking in a fortifying breath.

"I am finally able to forgive myself. I held onto my guilt for eight years. At last, I'm free." Her voice had softened, her eyes held a distant look. "I was a junior in college." Natasha stood up and began slowly walking around the table.

Sheila couldn't help but wonder if the girl was nervous, or if walking made telling her story easier.

"I met a senior name Greg Phillips. I fell hard for him. He wasn't handsome. He was attentive. He knew the right words to say to me. He told me I was beautiful and intelligent. I was an addict, needing to hear more from him." Natasha glanced at Mrs. Forester, who smiled and nodded. Natasha suddenly stopped, her eyes hardening briefly. "Somewhere in the relationship things changed. He lived off campus, and we had been dating for two months. The honeymoon stage was over. There were so many warning signals I ignored. The compliments were soon replaced by insults. His

117

attention was next to none. He just kept saying he was a man with needs and I was not meeting them." Natasha returned to her seat.

"Late one night, he called. It was 1 o'clock in the morning. He said that he needed me. My inner signals warned me not to go." A tear escaped, followed by another. Natasha didn't wipe them away. "I got there, and immediately he began kissing and touching me. It didn't feel right. He got angry and started calling me a tease. He pushed me to the floor. I started crying and screaming. He stopped and looked at me with such disgust and hatred. I didn't recognize him."

Natasha's eyes darted to each lady. Sheila's stomach knotted. "He got off of me, staggering to a chair. He told me I'd never be anybody, and the relationship was over. He told me that I was skinny and ugly and that no one would ever love me. Something in me died at that moment. My confidence was replaced with seeds of insecurity and doubt. I left the apartment; I went to my dorm room and told no one. I finished the semester, determined to get past the hurt. I graduated magna cum laude. Further my education; I received my advanced degree in Psychiatry. I couldn't celebrate or be proud of those things. I was empty.

"One day I was sitting in a park, and I saw a little girl crying. She said she couldn't find her mommy. I hugged the little girl close to me, promising to find her mommy. Something inside of me stirred to life. I felt like that little girl lost." The tears were now falling fast from Natasha's eyes. "If I had cried out or went to someone for help, I wouldn't have had to suffer alone. So much time wasted. I spent hours in that park looking for that little girl's mother. In the end, she found us. She had reported her daughter missing, and a small search party was sent out."

Sheila caught the exchanged between Natasha and Mrs. Forester again, it was subtle. Had she not been watching them, she would have missed it. She looked around at the table. The ladies were all wiping at their eyes.

"I forgive myself." Natasha began to repeat the words like they were a song. Soon, the ladies at the table joined in, Sheila included.

She found the more she said the words, the more liberated she was feeling. Her heart began to accelerate as she remembered her time growing up in the many foster homes. She felt like no one loved her, and that she wasn't good enough.

"I forgive myself," Sheila said, remembering the anger she harbored inside for being the victim of fate. Why her? Why was she not blessed with a father and mother, sisters and brothers? Many times she closed herself off to the world because of fear and doubt. "I forgive myself," she chanted over and over. "It wasn't my fault. I didn't ask to be born. To be left alone. I forgive myself." Sheila began to breathe heavily, her heart accelerating.

She felt a warm tingling sensation coursing through her body. It felt like someone had touched her. Looking around, she noticed that the ladies remained in their seats; their eyes were closed, their lips moving silently. Then there was calmness on the inside of her. She felt free and uplifted...empowered.

Mrs. Forester began to clap slowly and the rest of the ladies followed suit. "Chapter 5...forgiveness. What a wonderful page of life to be on. Thank you for a wonderful beginning, Natasha," she said.

Sheila smiled as Mrs. Montgomery grabbed her hand, squeezing it. "Forgiveness is a gift given to others by you; the gift of releasing negative entities from impeding your destiny." Mrs. Forester wisely proclaimed.

"I'm in a better place right now." Natasha shrugged her shoulders smiling. "I'm seeing someone special right now. We met in the Library. He is a professor at the local university." The ladies congratulated her, some even rising out of their chairs to embrace her.

"Ladies, ladies, please be seated, our time is up and we have yet to establish who shall add on to our chapter for next month. Oh, and Natasha dear, I'll look for my wedding invitation in the mail next year." Mrs. Forester winked conspiratorially. Natasha's eyes widened then she nodded, smiling radiantly.

"I would love to nominate our next contributor to our pages of life," Valerie stated.

"Of course, dear. Who might she be?" Mrs. Forester asked.

"Sheila Lawson," Valerie said. Sheila turned shocked eyes to Valerie.

Mother Montgomery clapped her hands exuberantly. "I will second that nomination. What an excellent choice, Valerie."

Sheila was all set to refuse until seven pairs of eyes landed on her. "Sure, I would love to be a contributor to the pages of life," she stated.

"Good, good. Well that settles it then, ladies. Until we meet again, stay full, stay focused and empowered women," Mrs. Forester said.

Sheila smiled, strangely she wasn't upset. She found that she wanted to tell her story with these ladies. She already knew the topic she would begin a page of life with...*Being Made Whole.* Already she felt a growing connection with them. If this was what is was like to feel empowered, then she wanted more.

Chapter 18

Mike and Sheila were in the park feeding the pigeons. She had finally finished adding the final touches to her painting. Mike had surprised her with a picnic for lunch. She was amazed at how at ease they began to fit into each other's lives. He purchased her a cell phone, one she had to be convinced to take at first.

He insisted that it was for his peace of mind. Not only was his numbers programmed, but his entire family and friends' numbers were programmed as well. He wanted to be available to her as much as possible. Sheila thought it was sweet and finally accepted the cell. When Mike released a long breath, it was then she became fully aware of how worried he was about her.

"I had a wonderful time today, Mike. I love spending time with you," Sheila said.

Mike brows lifted in delight. "Well, you're easy to please. If a picnic and my presence are wonderful to you, I think my job in making you happy will be easy," he said.

"You do make me happy. I have to ask myself if you are real at times."

Mike's expression became serious, his dark eyes searched hers. "I am real, Sheila. What I feel for you is real. Never doubt that. I see myself with you not just on Sundays, but everyday." Sheila swallowed hard under his penetrating gaze, not knowing what to say, she said nothing. "I think we better start packing up, sweetie. It looks like it's going to rain," Mike warned.
Sheila nodded softly; liking the endearment coming from Mike. Silently, acknowledging that; he was her sweetie too.

* * *

Mrs. Montgomery replaced the phone back on its cradle. She had preparing her menu for Sunday's dinner, when her friend, Estelle, called for her. Already there was talk of Mike and Sheila's blooming relationship. Mrs. Montgomery knew that information would soon leak out; she just had not expected it to be so soon.

She thought back to the dream she had of Mike running from his bride. She prayed that his demons from the past were buried, allowing him to move on and be happy with Sheila.

"You got that look in your eyes, Clara." Mr. Montgomery walked into the kitchen, gently kissing his wife on the cheek.

"Oh, and what look might that be, Pastor Montgomery?" she asked.

Mr. Montgomery settled himself across from his wife, pilfering one of her freshly baked blueberry muffins. "The one that says, someone is in trouble and I'm going to fix it," he murmured through a mouthful of muffin.

Mrs. Montgomery frowned at him with disapproval. She offered her husband a napkin. "Honey, please do not talk with your mouth full. Besides, I have no such 'look' as you say. You're making things up now." She looked down at her menu, adding to her grocery list things to purchase.

He remained silent, staring at his wife. "Clara," he warned, wiping at his mouth.

Mrs. Montgomery placed the menu down on the table. "Oh, all right, Estelle just called. It seems Mike and Sheila's relationship is the talk of the town."

"Well that doesn't surprise me. Although this is a large town, we have a fair amount of people who knows of us. Something like this can't stay hushed for long, Clara."

Sighing heavily, Mrs. Montgomery looked out the window. Two birds had landed. They were calling back and forward to each other, before taking flight to the sky.

"I know, I know. It's just that I wanted them to have a little more time together. Mike has endured so much. I have a feeling that Sheila has her own demons to fight as well. It's in her eyes. I just want to reach out and hold her tightly to me," she said.

Mr. Montgomery faced the love of his life. "If they are meant to be then can't no one or nothing keep them apart. We

Montgomery men take care of our own. All we can do is be there to support Mike and Sheila."

"And pray. I have a feeling they're going to need our prayers like never before," Mrs. Montgomery said.

Chapter 19

Sheila turned the car's engine off and allowed herself the luxury to reminisce. She and Mike had been dating for three glorious months. Looking into her rearview mirror, she smiled. They say that the eyes are the windows to the soul, hers held joy. But, for some reason, she was jittery and restless. She wanted to be free of the fear, however, could not. She could not help but feel that something was going to happen to cause her and Mike to break up. She was not voyeuristic by any means. However, she felt it.

Something was waiting in the horizon. She knew that her reservations were keeping their relationship from growing, but she couldn't help it. Mike was trying so hard to please her. Sighing, Sheila promised she would try extra hard to ignore these ominous feelings. If he was willing to fight for their love, then she was too.

She saw a movement from her peripheral vision. Looking out her car window, she saw nothing. She suddenly felt like she was being watched. Looking around for her purse, she hurriedly exited the car. She fumbled for her keys. She tripped, almost falling.

"I have got to get myself together," she said aloud.

"Ms. Lawson?"

Sheila screamed, dropping her keys. It was the young woman from the shelter. She was wearing her trademark dark clothing. There was something different about her. She looked emancipated. The dark circles under her eyes were indicative that she was not sleeping at all. The scent coming from her indicated she had not bathed in awhile.

"I'm sorry, I didn't mean to startle you," the woman said.

"Monica, you scared me half to death. How did you know where I lived?" Sheila bent to retrieve her fallen keys, missing the flash of pain crossing the young woman's face.

"I have my ways." Monica was fidgety. "Look, I can't stay long. I wanted to give you something."

"Would you like to come in? I could fix you something to eat." Sheila knew this was breaking work protocol, but something about the young woman called to her.

"No. I can't," Monica said in a teary voice.

Concerned, Sheila reached out to Monica, who immediately stepped back. Sheila allowed her hand to fall to her side, fearful Monica would run.

"I wanted to thank you for your help. You have restored a measure of faith in me." Tears pooled in her eyes. "For so long; I have been alone." Shrugging one slender shoulder, Monica said, "Except for this." She opened her hand, revealing a small black button. Sheila frowned at the button in confusion. Monica's thumb stroked the button gently. "This has been my only friend since I was ten."

Sheila's heart dropped at the soulful confession. She was always sensitive to the emotions of others. The need to help others is what influenced her job choice. She knew all too well the feeling of being alone. Having lived in a foster home her whole life, she often longed for a sister or a brother. She was very introverted as a child, trying to make friends was too much of an effort, so she never tried.

"This black button was more of a comfort than a friend really. I realize this now. I really have to go. They are after me." Sheila felt stark fear at her words. Monica was edgy tonight.

"Who is after you? Look, you do not have to run. I can get you the help you need..." Sheila stopped when Monica looked up. Her eyes were filled with such sorrow. "Tell me," she pleaded. Sheila could see Monica struggling with herself to tell the story.

"I can't." Opening her coat, Sheila was reminded that she was pregnant. Monica extended her hand.

"What is it?" Sheila asked.

"Read it and all will be revealed," Monica said, extending a small safe box to Sheila, who shook her head, refusing to take it.

"Why does this feel like goodbye, Monica?" Sheila asked.

"Because it is. Thank you."

"If you want to thank me, then please let me help you. We can go to the police," Sheila reasoned.

"No!"

The forceful denial stopped Sheila cold. Turning, she gasped at the wild look in Monica's eyes. "Monica, what's wrong? Why don't you want to involve the police in this?"

"Because, the police can not help me with this, I wish they could. If they could, I would have gone to them a long time ago."

"Look, Monica, from the beginning I tried to help you. I even jeopardized my job for you, and now it seems I may have even placed my life endanger. I think you own me an explanation," Sheila argued.

Monica pressed her hand to her protruding stomach. She stood there breathing in and out. She was whispering something low and guttural, the sound sounded ominous to Sheila. Sheila looked at Monica, really looked at her; finally noticing the pain lines itched on her face, and she was biting down hard on her lips.

Monica cried out, bending down at the waist. Sheila grabbed her around the waist, helping her to stand upright. She felt Monica stiffen.

"What is it, Monica? What's wrong?" Sheila asked.

My water just broke!" Monica cried.

Sheila shook her head vigorously. "We have to get you to a hospital."

"No, no hospital." Monica was panting hard now, beads of sweat dotting her forehead. "We have to deliver the baby here."

"No way, Monica. I don't know how to deliver a baby. We have to get you to a hospital." Sheila reiterated.

"Then you might as well kill me and my baby now. Because we're dead if we go to the hospital." Monica screamed from the pain.

Sheila wanted to cry and laugh at the same time. How did she come to be in such a situation? She did not know anything about delivering babies. Sure see watched *The Delivery Channel*. But this wasn't TV, this was real life.

Feeling herself panicking, Sheila began to breathe in and out. She offered up a quick prayer. *Jesus, I need help. I cannot do this alone. Please, help us.*

She didn't know if it was her imagination, but she could hear the words from the Bible. *I can do all things through Christ, which strengthens me.* She clung to that Bible verse. She was suddenly reminded of the Christmas story, *How the Grinch Stole Christmas.* The Grinch's heart was small, making him insensitive and uncaring of others. But as he realized the wrongness of his deeds; his heart began to grow. He wanted to right the wrongness of his dastardly deeds.

Suddenly warmth began to spread through her, and as she continued to repeat the Bible verse, her faith began to grow. She could do this. She would do this. Monica and her baby would survive.

"Okay, let's bring your baby into the world," She said, and she meant it.

* * *

Mike was just finishing recording his last court documentation report so that his secretary could transcribe it and file it away for him. Stretching, his rumbling stomach reminded him that it was lunchtime. He was suddenly overwhelmed to see Sheila. He would surprise her with lunch.

Warming to the idea, he called *Mia Bella,* his favorite Italian restaurant. After placing two orders, he decided to call Sheila's house, to inform her that he was coming over. His mama raised him right, he knew better than to drop in on a lady unexpectedly. Mike replaced the phone after hearing Sheila's voicemail. He would try again later. He collected his items and exited his office.

Chapter 20

Rayna was numbed with disbelief. Three weeks had passed since her telephone call with her mystery man. His presence seemed to intensify with the passage of time. She could recall more details of their meeting. Without effort, he seemed to have etched his way into her thoughts, interrupting her daily functions.

This was one of the reasons she shied away from relationships and commitments, whatever the term is for this new millennium. The emotional attachments, she didn't think she was ready for that yet. *Damaged goods*. Unwanted, the familiar words came. It was like a cold bucket of water being splashed on her. A Cardinal landed on the top of her car hood. It cried out, looking around. It looked directly at Rayna for a brief moment, and Rayna felt like it was trying to communicate with her. It then took off into the sky, circling high. Glancing up, she was humbled by the billowy clouds. Inhaling, she offered up a prayer of guidance.

"Alright, I'm going to need a little guidance here. Why can I not shake this man from my mind?" Rayna rested her head against the steering wheel.

She was struck by how beautiful downtown looked after some re-gentrification. She remembered the great debate between the upper class and the lower class, the rich wanting to expand, bringing more business to the area. The lower class wanted the youth things to remain as they were. The debate made headlines both nationally and locally. There was a phenomenal protest as the right to their beloved community united people from all walks of life. In the end, the big dogs won out, thus new businesses and more congested parking areas.

One of those businesses was a success soul food restaurant named Rosa Dell's. It was featured twice in Black Enterprise Magazine. Several prominent celebrities often patronized; the quaint restaurant. The $10.00, sandwich Rayna was feasting on was purchased from there.   Rayna confessed it was well worth every penny.

Turning, she recognized a familiar car...Eric's car. Not ready to face him yet, she hastily slid lower in her seat. Eric emerged from his car and her heart skipped a beat. Her sandwich was forgotten. Her vow to put him out of her mind was forgotten. She was flooded with memories, and this time, she embraced them.

He was handsome in his navy blue pinned-striped suit. His hair was freshly cut, and his goatee was neatly trimmed. The word 'confidence' came to mind. Rayna, swallowing hard, was praying that he wouldn't discover her hiding place. Eric suddenly stopped and looked around, as if sensing something. Rayna slid further down into her seat, holding her breath.

A stunningly beautiful woman, with a short cut, emerged from the restaurant, embracing Eric. She was an exact replica of the actress Salli Richardson. Eric smiled, mouthing something. The woman leaned her head to the side, causing a lock of hair to fall in her eye. Eric brushed the errant strand of hair behind the woman's ear.

Even from the distance, Rayna could see the woman's pronounced dimples. She was slender, elegantly dressed in a white two-piece pantsuit. Jimmy Choo shoes graced her feet. They both turned, and entered the sophisticated restaurant. Pausing, Eric looked around again, as if looking for something or someone. Rayna's breathe hitched, she waited. Mike's trained eyes scanned the area one last time, before finally turning to enter the restaurant.

Rayna slowly set up, her sandwich falling to the car floor. It didn't matter, she was no longer hungry. So that was it. He couldn't have a relationship with her because he was already in one. She could possibly well be his wife. Rayna suddenly became angry with herself. *Stupid. Stupid.* Turning the key in the ignition, she resolved to leave Eric and their chance encounter behind.

In the restaurant, Eric paused in mid-sentence.

"What is it, Eric?" The woman followed his gaze. She could see nothing out of the ordinary.

Clearing his throat, Eric smiled at his baby sister. "I thought I saw someone I knew."

"From the looks of things it must be a woman," his sister said.

"Why must it be a woman?" he asked.

"Because, big brother, you have this look about you lately. It's a man who's in love kind of look."

Eric choked on the water he was drinking. "Whoa there, half pint. That's a powerful statement; wrong though it may be." His sister only laughed, gently offering him a napkin. "I'm not in love. One would have to be in a relationship to be in love and I am not. So, end of story," he rationalized.

"I think that the man does protest too much."

"Look, Erica, sister of mine. If I were in love, which I am not by the way, I would tell you. But I will confess to you, oh little nosy one," Erica laughed out loud in response, "that I did meet someone briefly. I thought that I saw her pass by just now." Eric nodded toward the window.

Leaning forward with excitement, Erica smiled, rubbing her hands together. "Okay, now we're getting somewhere. Details, I need all the details, leave nothing out. What does she look like? Do I know her?" Eric leaned back in his seat, smiling secretively. Erica's eyes narrowed. "Please don't make me reach across this table, Eric." Her brother's secret smiled remained. "You are so wrong. You know I have to live my life vicariously through you."

"That, little sister, is entirely your fault. It's not healthy the amount of time you spend traveling. If I didn't know any better, I'd say you were running." Eric was referring to her current position of being an airline stewardess.

It seemed all her career choices required her to travel outside the country for extensive time periods. Erica was pricked by Eric's words, as they hit close to home. Maybe she was running, but this wasn't about her, she resolved, it was about her twin. She would deal with her issues later.

Erica flung her long silky locks over one slender shoulder in exasperation.

"And I'd say to you, older brother, that you don't know what you're talking about." She abruptly held up one hand. "Stop trying to distract me. Who is she?"

"She's someone I can't have. And therefore, there is no reason to further discuss her," Eric said, his voice lowering in warning.

Shaking her head slowly, Erica leaned forward. "When are you going to stop punishing yourself? It wasn't your fault. That witch is to blame. May her soul rot in hell for all eternity and..." her voice trailed off, as she noticed the muscle jumping in Eric's face, a sure indication that he was upset. "I'm sorry, Eric. Look, I just want at least one of us to be happy." Her eyes began to mist up. "God knows we deserve some happiness in our lives."

Eric reached across the table, squeezing his sister's hand in comfort. "Her name is Rayna." He cleared his throat, his memory of her causing a dull ache in his chest. Unconsciously, he began to rub his chest. Erica caught the action, this time she smiled secretively.

"Truthfully, I know little about her. She was caught in a rainstorm and I gave her a ride home." Eric leaned back in his chair. "The problem is I can't get her out of my mind." His voice softened in memory. He shook his head, as if clearing it. "I thought I saw her pass by moments ago."

Erica knew her brother. He was not transparent with his feeling. Getting him to open up about himself was like pulling teeth. When Eric allowed you into his heart and world, you couldn't have a better friend and confidante. She wanted to meet this Rayna, the woman who was causing ripples and waves in her brother's normally calm river.

"Rayna," Erica tested the name. "I like it." She nodded in approval. "And for her to leave such a lasting impression on you, in such a short time, is indicative that she is going to be your wife. For the second time that day, Eric choked on his water. "Wife? You really have lost it, little one."

Erica retrieved her blackberry from her purse. Clicking on her calendar, she hastily keyed in something. Eric just watched his baby sister in amazement.

"Nope, you'll see. I bet around this time next year, your Rayna will be my sister-in-law." Closing her blackberry with a snap, she smiled triumphantly at her brother. Eric couldn't help it; he returned his sister's smile, poor thing. But she was in for a great disappointment.

He was certain he would never marry. He couldn't. It wasn't part of the creator's plan for him. Married? Mentally, he tested the word. For that to happen, there must be a relationship, and he was in no way going to form one with Rayna. Rayna was the type of woman you make a home with; two cars, two point three children, and a white picket fence, a fairy tale life. He didn't believe such happiness existed for him. Trouble seemed to follow him. No, it was better for him to stay away from Rayna, she deserved better. Now, if only his heart would listen to his mind.

Erica's soft laughter lulled him from his silent ruminations. "Oh yeah, around this time next year, big brother, your Rayna will be my sister-in-law. Cheers." She saluted Eric with her water glass.

"We will see," he said, returning her smile and saluting with his water.

Chapter 21

Sheila looked at the mounds of towels and boiled water, realizing she didn't have the slightest idea what to do with them. She remembered those items mentioned on TV.

"I'm sorry I brought you into this," Monica said sadly.

Sheila's heart sank at the pitiful confession. Monica was lying on the sofa, with several pillows supporting her from behind. She was rapidly breathing in and out; it was obvious she was in pain. Her face was slightly pale, and she was sweating profusely. Sheila knelt down in front of Monica. Taking a damp rag, she began to wipe at the fast falling sweat.

"You just concentrate on bringing your baby into the world. Save your energy, you're going to need it soon," Sheila said.

The unexpected loud sound of thunder caused both women to jump. Sheila calmly glanced at Monica, as her insides were all scrambled. She had to remain calm for the both of them. For the millionth time, she wished Mike was there with her. She jumped up and went to the window.

Of late, it seemed all it has been doing was storming and raining. It was so dark outside. The dark clouds gave the world a gray cast. Sheila looked at the clock on the mantel. It was only 6 o'clock pm.

"Where did this storm come from?" Sheila asked aloud.

She felt the formation of chill bumps on her arms. She couldn't shake the feeling that something bad was going to happen. She looked around at her beloved neighborhood. She lived in a cul-de-sac neighborhood with a 19th century charm to it. Her neighborhood seemed like a different place this night.

Her elderly neighbors, Mr. and Mrs. Honeycutt, were out of town visiting their only daughter; who'd just had a baby a couple of days ago. Maybe their being out of town was what was causing the disconnect feeling. Still, Sheila couldn't help but to feel that something was not right. Every nerve ending told her so.

LOVE FOUND ME

"Something is not right." Hearing Monica voice her thoughts aloud, caused Sheila to turn sharply at Monica. Feeling a sense of foreboding was one thing, but to have someone else voice it aloud was just too unsettling.

"What do mean? Everything is going to be all right, sweetie. You're getting ready to bring life into this world; it can't get any better than that." Sheila laughed softly, trying to sound brave.

Sheila returned to Monica, slowly wiping away the ever forming perspiration. Monica frowned; she tried to say something but was cut off by another contraction. She was forced to continue breathing in and out.

"Don't handle me. Please respect me enough to be real with me." Sheila held the younger woman's stare. Maybe if she pretended she didn't know what she was talking about, all this would just fade away. The sound of the thunder dispelled that theory. Their situation was very much real, and no amount of pretending was going to change that.

"Who are you?" Sheila asked.

"I am not crazy and neither are you, Sheila. What we are however is in danger. I'm sorry I brought you into this, but I had nowhere else to go. The voice sent me here to you," Monica said.

"What are you talking about, Monica? What voice?" Sheila felt unadulterated fear, now certain that she was harboring an insane woman in her home.

"I am not crazy." Monica echoed the words again, as if trying to convince herself this time.

Sheila felt herself growing angry. She was chartering grounds she'd never been before. She was certain that Monica was hiding answers she needed, and yet was slow in rendering them, causing her to become irate. If she was willing to go to bat for her, surely Monica could give her some straight forth answers. Because, without a doubt, she was definitely in trouble, and from the sound of things, she was too. Sheila was determined to find out what it was. Question was, was she ready to handle the truth?

Standing, Sheila walked slowly to the mantel to a picture of her smiling in a white one-piece bathing suit. She looked like a model for a campaign ad. She had been vacationing in Hawaii. It was her very first vacation out of the country by herself. She wished she could return to that day of tranquility and new beginnings.

"You're talking about voices. You're on the run from heaven knows who or what, and you're not giving me any answers." Sheila slowly approached Monica. "Enough. This cat and mouse game must end tonight. You owe me some answers, and I want them now."

At first, Sheila thought her demand would go unanswered, as Monica continued to breathe. They held each other's stare.

Finally, Monica spoke. "I'm being hunted." She stopped talking, her gaze going blank. She suddenly nodded, as if hearing something.

"Monica? Hunted by whom?" Sheila asked.

Monica slowly turned, facing Sheila. "Years ago, unbeknownst to her, my mother married into a secret organization. More like a cult really. They only mingle with the outside world to work. They marry within their society."

Sheila sat down on the soft sofa, sensing that her world was about to change with the story Monica was telling her. She almost stopped her from telling her the rest, but knew she couldn't help the young woman unless she knew the whole story.

"My mother was beautiful and rich." Monica laughed bitterly. "Ridiculously rich. She was an only child and very spoiled. My mother didn't get along with my grandparents, she thought they were controlling." She paused, squeezing the pillow tightly, breathing in and out.

"This baby is ready for the world," Sheila said.

Monica rubbed her protruding belly. "Soon, little one, soon."

"Monica, I still think we should get you to a hospital." Sheila's brows furrowed with worry.

Monica continued on as if Sheila had not spoken. Her voice had dropped an octave; Sheila had to lean in closer to hear her words. "My mother was an extraordinary beautiful woman. She could have had anyone she wanted. One day, my mother met a man. That shouldn't sound so unusual, but it was how she met him that was unusual for my mother. She met him at a church function." Monica peered at the Bible resting on Sheila's coffee table. "He was handsome and well mannered. My mother was accustomed to men fawning all over her. Needless to say, she was a bit miffed that this stranger had not shown the slightest interest in her." Monica paused, as if listening to something.

She nodded her head, continuing her story. "My mother was determined to have this man, and whatever mama wanted, she got. Only this time she got more than what she bargained for. He was a snake in disguise. Words were his weapon, and he knew exactly how to use them. A young naïve woman like my mother didn't stand a chance. Their courtship was fast and furious. They quickly married with my grandparents consent. My mother took her inheritance, and together she and my father moved to another state."

Sheila felt like she was listening to something out of a suspense novel, it all seemed surreal.

"My father's whole demeanor changed. He forbade my mother to have any contact with the outside world, my grandparents especially. Mama rebelled at first, but in the end, she lost her will to fight. My father was verbally and mentally abusive to her. Calling her half a woman, because it had been four years and she had yet to conceive. Finally, when she did conceive, he was ecstatic. Even more so when he discovered I was a girl."

"Why would your being a girl make your father excited? A baby should be cherished regardless of its gender." Sheila voice hardened with anger.

Monica smiled through the pain that was gripping her. "Because girls are what they call 'breeders'. We were to breed the ultimate seed that would unite all their kind." She laughed bitterly. "The story is that many years ago a young woman and man fell dangerously in love. She was what they called 'pure blood'."

"Pure Blood? I hate to tell you this, Monica, but over the years, the races of the world have mingled. Is there such as thing as pure blood anymore?"

"Your point is, duly noted. But by pure blood, I mean a virgin." Monica inhaled sharply.

"How disgusting, and not to mention judgmental. What a warped way of thinking," Sheila said.

"Be that as it may, it is what it is. These people have no hearts. They are demented. It's true as you stated, they are warped in their way of thinking. They break into the homes of the innocent. They torture and rape women and steal their female child, making them breeders." Monica's voice sounded robotic. "And they did all of this as my father watched."

"Your father?" Sheila asked shocked. The howling winds reminded her of a wounded animal's cry. The window and doors were shaking under its assault.

Monica winched as another contraction hit. "It was late one night. The voice spoke to me, warning me to leave, but I couldn't---wouldn't leave mother. I loved and hated my mother." She rubbed her protruding stomach, as if comforting her unborn child. "I could not say that before. I always thought of her as weak. I realized later how strong she really was," she said, with a small smile forming. "In her own way, she protected me. She would have never survived had she left my father. There are just too many of them, and they are powerful and evil."

Monica and Sheila screamed at the sound of a loud crashing noise. The living room window had flung open; the room's warmth was overpowered by the cold winds. Sheila ran to the window, closing and locking it.

"The wind has picked up," Sheila said.

Sheila began to tremble, chill bumps once again forming on her arms, only it wasn't from the cold. Something was not right tonight. Turning, she peered out the window again. The darkness was frightening. Even the stars and the moon hid themselves.

"The prophecy spoke of a man and woman one day uniting, and when this union takes place, their people would take their rightful place in this heathen world," Monica continued.

Sheila turned slowly, facing Monica. "You called them a sect. Does this sect have a name?" she asked.

"They do. They are called Zion." Monica stilled suddenly.

Sheila ran and knelt down in front of her, thinking something was wrong with the baby. "What is it? Is it the baby?"

"We have to get out here. The voice has spoken," Monica said.

"The voice? What are talking about? What voice?" Sheila briefly wondered if Monica was mental. Looking into Monica's eyes, she saw something; fear and determination. No, she wasn't insane. She was however in trouble, and now so was she. They were being hunted.

Monica was trying to get up from her position but couldn't. Sheila reached down, helping her to her feet.

"What is going on, Monica?"

"They have found us. We have to go now!"

"I'm calling the police; this is too big for us to handle alone." Panic stricken, Sheila ran to the phone. The sound of a door slamming caused her to paused dialing.

"It's too late, they're here. We have to get out of here," Monica said.

Sheila went to window and peered out. There was a dark car with dark tinted windows parked across the street from her house. A man dressed in black was bent over talking to someone in the back. Slowly, the door opened and a tall man dressed in black exited the car. Not once did he take his eyes off the house. Slowly wiping his mouth with a small black cloth, he smiled, looking directly into Sheila's eyes. Standing, Sheila could swear she was looking into the eyes of evil. The man's sardonic smile caused her to hastily backpedal.

"We have to get out of here now," Sheila said urgently.

"Is there a backdoor?" Monica was wobbling towards the back of the house. "It's too late. I'm sure they have this place surrounded by now. He has come for us." She looked around for a weapon.

"Us? What do you mean us?" Sheila asked.

"I wanted to tell you at the right time. Now I'm not so certain if there will ever be a right time. Sheila, I have been following you for years. I just never knew how to approach you."

Sheila stiffened, sensing the next words from Monica would drastically change her life forever.

"I'm your sister," Monica said.

There it was; the final missing piece. Sheila was stunned. She looked at Monica really hard. They didn't look anything alike. Her nose was small and pert. Monica's was full. Their skin coloring was opposite; hers was a creamy brown and Monica's was a vanilla. Looking closer, Sheila could see it in the eyes. They had the same almond shaped eyes.

"But how? I don't understand?" Sheila asked, still not believing that Monica was her sister.

Monica smiled softly." We have the same father, and for that, I am sorry. Our father was one of those sick men who married women in the name of Zion. You're not the only one. There are others."

"You mean I have more sisters and brothers out there?"

"Yes. You're the only one I have been able to find so far. In my safe box is information leading to the others," Monica said.

"Stop calling them the others. You make them sound like aliens or something." Sheila knew she sounded harsh, but this whole ordeal seemed like something out of a Stephen King book. It was making her act out of character. She stiffened as a thought formed. "Monica? Who is the father of your child?"

Instantly Monica's whole demeanor suddenly changed. Her eyes hardened, and her lips began moving rapidly. For a moment, Sheila barely recognized her. The sound of someone turning her front door handle spurred her into action.

She grabbed Monica's hand, and whispered, "Sorry, but we don't have time for a family bonding right now. Looks like my questions will have to wait. We have to survive first. Come on."

Monica followed Sheila into the bedroom. Sheila was determined that she and her sister would survive. *Sister.* Sheila tried the word out. She would have to get acclimated to that notion. Rayna was the closest thing she had to a family. Now she had a sister. There were too many unanswered questions.

"Wait!" Monica swung her backpack on her shoulder. "My safe box, I have to get it."

"We don't have time, Monica. Remember, you gave me your safe box, and I hid it in a safe place. We can come back for it later. Now move!" Sheila demanded.

Once they reached her bedroom, Sheila locked her bedroom door. She dropped to her knees, reached her right hand under the bed, and began moving her hand back and forth, as if looking for something.

Monica watched Sheila; afraid that fear was causing Sheila to momentarily lose focus. Suddenly Monica leaped back; gasped in amazement, as she watched a floor panel slide open about a foot from where she was standing by the dresser drawer, revealing a small hidden door.

Sheila leaped up, ran to her dresser drawer, where she retrieved both her cell phone and car keys. Once again she grabbed Monica by the hand, who arched a thin brow in question.

"The person who built this house was a slave abolitionist. He built this house to help run away slaves seek freedom. It was the main reason why I purchased this house. Cost me an exorbitant amount of money. I knew I had to buy it, but didn't think I'd need it one day."

The sound of the front door crashing open caused both women to shriek out loud. Sounds of their assailants' heavy foot steps could be heard. Sheila could hear the door rattling as someone turned the knob. Their assailants' wasn't even trying to be subtle.

"Let's go," Sheila said quietly.

Once they entered through the small door on the floor, Sheila pressed another button on the sidewall, and the door silently closed, encasing them in utter darkness. Monica screamed. Sheila immediately clamped her hand over her mouth. Monica began to struggle.

"Monica, you've got to control your fear or else we're dead," Sheila whispered desperately.

Monica whimpered softly, nodding her head in understanding. Sheila waited a couple of seconds before she released her.

"I'm afraid of small places," Monica confessed.

Sheila could hear the panic in Monica's voice, and her heart went out to the young woman. Although they were underground, sound still carried.

"Monica, just breathe. If you scream they will hear you then we're dead. Control it." A wide-eyed Monica nodded her head vigorously. "There are some flashlights down here."

Immediately Monica began to breathe in and out. "Sorry, I'm all right now. I'm going to have this baby and soon, Sheila." Monica covered her eyes as bright light filled the small tunnel.

"Sorry," Sheila said.

"Let's just get out of here, please," Monica said, her voice trembling with fear.

Taking Monica by the hand, Sheila led her further down the small corridor, where there was the smell of damp earth assaulting their nostrils. She could hear the sound of little critters, and she had to force her mind to go blank. She was deathly afraid of rats, and now was not the time to panic.

Sheila could hear the intruders above them. They were in her kitchen directly above them. Objects crashing to the floor above them caused both her and Monica to jump.

Sheila motioned for Monica to be quiet. Sheila listened, following the sound of their intruders' feet above them. They were heading towards her bedroom.

"Come on, we've got to move."

Monica bit down hard on her lip, drawing blood. "I have to push! I can't take it any longer, I am so sorry. I have to push!" Monica cried.

"No, Monica, please, we have to get out of here. Just a little bit further and we'll be outside." Sheila's heart dropped as Monica slid heavily to the floor.

At a loss as what to do, she dropped heavily beside Monica, silently sending up a prayer of guidance and protection. Patting her pant pocket, Sheila was comforted by the small gun she carried. She detested guns of any sort, but as a single woman living alone, she was advised by Rayna, who also carried one, to purchase one as a safety measure. Together, they registered for their permits to carry a weapon and took target lessons. Sheila was happy she'd listen to Rayna for once. She was determined that both she and her sister would make it through the night.

Chapter 22

Something was not right. Mike couldn't quite put his finger on it. It was more of a feeling really. When he was a kid, he used to get these feelings when something bad was about to happen. Bryan called them his spider senses.

One day, he and Bryan were at the park playing baseball. All of a sudden, the feeling of sadness overcame him. The need to cry was heavy. Finally, telling Bryan how he was feeling, they went home. The sound of their mother crying sent them running into the living room. It was there they saw their father hugging their mother.

"Mom?" they both asked.

"Boys come in. We need to talk." Their father's voice was soft, a sure indication something was amiss.

Their mother nodded her head at her husband. Mike and Bryan walked with heavy limbs into their living room. Their mother had decorated the room with brown and cream colors. She said the room was designed to bring comfort. Today, it felt anything but warming.

Clearing his throat, their father began. "Today your grandmother, Lucille, died." Mike and Bryan simultaneously glanced at each other.

Ever since then, Mike learned to listen to his warning signals. Today, his senses were going amok. Something was not right.

He dialed his brother's number.

"Tell me something good, little brother." Bryan's voice sounded chipper.

"It's all good, big man. I was calling to remind you about the art exhibit next Saturday," Mike said.

"You need not worry about it. The whole crew will be there in support of you and your lady."

"Thanks, man. Sheila is extraordinarily nervous; the show of support will help her relax some."

Bryan chuckled lightly. "I'm sure you will benefit from the support as well."

Mike smiled, his brother knew him well. "Dido that. Look, have you spoken with Mom and Pop today?"

"Yes, I did. They were both at the gym. Mom found out Pop's cholesterol was high, and immediately went into nurse mode. She has changed their meal plan, and formed an exercising routine for the both of them." Mike chuckled softly.

"I'm sure Pop loves every moment of it," Bryan said, also laughing.

"Like a dog loves water." Mike smiled after hanging up with his brother.

All was well with the family. Yet something was not right. Mike picked his cell up again, dialing Sheila's number. He snapped it shut after hearing Sheila's voicemail. Making a sharp left turn, heading toward I40, he prayed everything was all right.

Chapter 23

"I can't move. This baby is ready to come into the world," Monica cried.

"Okay then, let's give her what she wants." Sheila knelt down beside Monica, freeing her from her tattered jeans.

"Her? How do you know it's a girl?" Monica asked between labored breathe.

Sheila set back on her haunches. "Call it women's intuition." She winked.

Monica tried to laugh, but moaned loudly instead. Sheila was worried, she never had a child, but she was pretty sure those moans would soon turn into a screaming fest, alarming their intruders to their location.

Tearing her shirt, Sheila rolled it up and handed it to Monica. "Here, bite down hard on this," she said. Monica immediately placed the cloth in her mouth, as another contraction hit. "Okay, Monica, breathe in and out." It was easier said than done, with the cloth in her mouth.

It was hot in the small tunnel. Both Monica and Sheila were both drenched with sweat. The sound of crickets and other unidentified sounds were playing havoc on Sheila's already frayed nerves.

The baby was slow in coming. Monica had been pushing for sometime now, and the baby refused to come. Sheila, wiping at the fast falling sweat from Monica's eyes, began to worry. Monica wasn't looking good. Her face was paler than before. There was a trickle of blood on the side of her mouth, and her lips were swollen from biting hard on them. Sheila's back was hurting something fierce and her legs where numb from kneeling down so long.

Monica spit the cloth out of her mouth. "I have got to rest, I'm tired," she said, her voice sounding hoarse. Sheila nodded. She needed a break herself.

Standing, she stretched, sighing loudly. Leaning her head to the side, she listened. Their stalkers had grown quiet, but she knew they were still upstairs waiting. They wouldn't give up that easily. Sheila turned sharply at Monica's cry. Repositioning herself between Monica's legs, she was surprised to see the baby's head.

"Oh my goodness, I can see the head! Push, Monica, push, your baby wants out!" Sheila demanded.

Monica placed the cloth back into her mouth, trying valiantly to bring life into the world. Her face was pinched with pain. Her swollen lips were moving, but nothing was coming out. Frantically swinging her head from side to side, Monica spit the cloth out her mouth.

"I can't do it." Monica's weak voice caused Sheila's heart to drop. "I'm too tired. I can't push anymore."

Sheila raked her hands through her thick dark tresses, sending them into wild disarray. Leaning back on her haunches, at a loss for words, she simply stared at Monica. Monica just continued to breathe in and out stubbornly, holding her stare. Sheila felt like screaming, she was angry with Monica, but mostly angry with herself.

Was this what happens when one wanted to save the world? You get crazy cult people wanting to take over the world, possibly losing out on the love of your life, and a newfound pregnant sister who refused to deliver her own child.

A sound escaped Sheila. First, it sounded like a gurgle. Then it erupted like lava spewing from a volcano. Sheila couldn't stop laughing, it was a frightening sound.

"Sheila." Monica's voice was shocked and greatly alarmed.

Sheila heard Monica's voice from a distance, but couldn't stop laughing. Was this what it felt like to go insane? She couldn't stop laughing. Her side was beginning to hurt, her eyes were watering, and she could barely catch her breath. Sheila suddenly felt a sharp sting on her face. It took a moment for what just transpired to sink in.

"You slapped me," Sheila said.

"I'm sorry. You were panicking and it was the right thing to do," Monica said.

Sheila stared wide-eyed at Monica, blinking twice. Finally, she nodded her head.

"I saw that on a television show once. I never believed in the method." Monica shrugged her slender shoulders.

"It worked." Sheila rubbed her stinging cheek. Monica nodded, leaning back against the wall. She began breathing in and out.

Sheila could hear the sound of rats crawling in the dark cavern, but she wasn't afraid of them anymore. The damp earth was causing her pants to stick to her and she was cold. She thought about Mike, he was her light. She remembered his strength and focused on it.

Closing her eyes, she leaned back against the wall. Remembering their first meeting, she was no longer that introversive woman running from love. Love found her, and she was determined to live the happy ending she knew she was destined for.

Whenever he looked at her, she felt like a woman. He made her feel loved and needed. His spirit and his generosity were incomparable. Her insecurities almost lost out on a great man. She had to deal with her low self-esteem. Mike never lied to her ever. If he said he loved her, then he loved her.

"I am so sorry, Mike. I am so sorry," Sheila said.

"You're in love." Monica made it a statement and not a question.

Sheila's eyes remained closed; she didn't want to lose the image of Mike.

"When I get out of here, I'm going to let him know in every way possible how much I do."

Sheila went perfectly still. She smelled it before she saw it. It was smoke! The house was on fire. This galvanized her into action. She scrambled over to Monica, gripping her arms firmly.

"You're going to deliver your baby. You're almost there. Push just a little harder. You can do it, Monica! Do it because you want to live to raise your child, and I want my family to survive. My niece is ready to live, Monica. Help her live." Sheila softened her voice.

Monica tried pushing, but gave up after the second push. "I can't do it. I don't have the energy." Her baby's head was almost out; Sheila could see the dark matted hair.

"Listen to me! You've come too far to give up now. I'm not asking you to push, I'm telling you to push! My niece is ready to live. I didn't take you for a weak woman, Monica. You really had me fooled. A real woman would give it all she's got to bring life into the world," Sheila said, hoping to urge Monica to push her baby out.

Sheila prayed God would forgive her for those stinging words, but she was at a loss with what else to do. Monica stared hard at Sheila, panting hard. Reaching for the discarded cloth, Monica clamped down hard on it and began to push, screaming hard through the cloth.

"That's it, Monica! Come on, baby, come on. The head is out, push!" Sheila grabbed the baby as it slid out. "It's a girl! It's a beautiful girl!" She took off her sweater, and wrapped the baby in it. She held her gently, smiling at the miracle in her arms. Monica looked exhausted, but was smiling. Sheila gave the infant to Monica.

"She is beautiful," Monica said.

"Just like her mother," Sheila said.

Monica continued to look at her daughter with tears running down her cheeks. "Hello baby. I want you to know that I love you, and that I will protect you with my dying breath. You are my miracle." She softly kissed the squirming newborn. "I'm going to name you Miracle. You are my miracle."

"I need something to cut the umbilical cord with." Sheila was looking around.

"I have a box knife in my backpack," Monica announced, without looking up.

Sheila reached for the worn bag, retrieved the knife, and severed the umbilical cord.

"Monica, I'm sorry, sweetie, but we can't stay here. They've set the house on fire. The smoke alone can kill us if we stay. We have to keep moving," Sheila said.

"I understand. I will do whatever it takes for my baby, but I truly don't know how far I can make it. I'm just so weak."

"We're going to make it." Sheila smiled, realizing she meant it.

Monica heard the secret door open. Their time was up, they had been discovered.

Chapter 24

Mike, once again retrieved his cell. Punching in a familiar number, he prayed his contact would answer.

"Hello," a familiar voice answered.

"Man, I need your help," Mike said.

"Tell me what you need."

Mike felt a little calmer. He knew he was talking to one of the best investigators in the world, highly trained in weaponry, courtesy of the special ops force. Mike never thought he'd be calling on his friend to utilize his skills on his behalf. He never thought his life would take a turn like it had. If anything happened to Sheila, he knew he would never be the same again. He refused to let anything happen to her.

"I think Sheila may be in danger. I don't have concrete evidence. I have 'a feeling', man." Mike waited for his words to sink in. His childhood friend would understand what he meant. Only he and Bryan knew about these premonitions.

"I'm on my way over to her house," Mike said.

"Give me the address, I'll meet you there." It was a command.

Mike gave him the address before hanging up. He pressed down on the accelerator. "Hold on baby, I'm coming. Fight for us." He sent up another prayer for protection.

* * *

Rayna lingered over her now lukewarm cup of coffee. She set staring out the café's window. The rain was falling hard and fast, reminding her of the fateful day she met Eric. It seemed everything of late reminded her of him. She wondered if he were right now having a candlelight dinner with the beautiful woman she'd seen him with. Who was she? Was she his wife or girlfriend?

"Gal, don't you know frowning cause's line marks on your face?"

Rayna jumped at the familiar voice. "Mother Hattie?"

"And you've got such a beautiful face too. Ain't any need adding wrinkles to your face this early, they'll come soon enough. Trust me, I should know." Mother Hattie nodded at the empty seat. "Do you mind if I rest my feet a spell?"

Rayna jumped up. "Please do sit. I would love the company."

Mother Hattie slid her frame into the comfortable booth. "Ahh yes, this feels mighty good. What a beautiful day it is."

Rayna smiled softly, looking out the window again. "Mother Hattie, it's raining cats and dogs out." The rain continued its heavy descent.

Oddly, despite the weather's temperament, Rayna felt a sense of warmth. Maybe the presence of Mother Hattie had something to do with it.

Rayna opened her mouth about to question Mother Hattie for being out in such dour weather, but paused as a server came to take Mother Hattie's order.

"Just a cup of tea for me, little lamb chowder," Mother Hattie said. Rayna requested a refill on her cup of coffee. "See, some people can't see the good in the storm," Mother Hattie said. "Wisdom comes with age. Knowledge comes with experience, and understanding comes with a willing mind."

Rayna was completely enthralled, captured by the soothing words of Mother Hattie. She leaned in closer, sensing there was a lesson to be learned.

"What do you mean, Mother Hattie?" Rayna asked.

"Looking at you, precious, I'd wager it is the latter you need." Mother Hattie raised one hand, cutting off Rayna's denial. "You don't have to say a word to me. I'm too old not to discern a situation. I been through just about all there is to experience. I need to write one of them... uh, what you call 'em? Nonfiction books about my life. Probably hit the New York Times best seller list in the first week of its release." Mother Hattie began squirming in her seat. "I got some nosy friends, always wanting to know about my life." She winked conspirationally. "I ain't been good all my life, little sweet pea, but that is another story. Tell me what got you frowning so, little angel of the field?"

Rayna couldn't help but smile at the name. Mother Hattie's unexpected presence was a blessing, because she really did need someone to share her feelings with. Why not Mother Hattie?

Their server returned with their requested orders. Rayna circled the rim of her coffee cup with her finger and shrugged.

"Well, it's complicated. I think I'm in love with a stranger." Laughing nervously, Rayna leaned back in her seat, staring out the window. A couple was running to their car. The man opened up the passenger's side door for his companion, then scurried to his side. All the while, he was smiling despite the heavy downpour. *Love,* Rayna thought to herself.

"That I might be in love with a stranger is ridiculous, because we have only met once, and spoken over the phone once." Rayna knew she was rambling, but couldn't stop herself.

"For some people, it only takes one time to fall in love," Mother Hattie said.

"Love!" To self confess it was one thing, but to have someone tell her sent a shockwave to her system. Rayna's outcry garnered them several stares. She nodded an apology. She leaned closer to Mother Hattie whispering, "No, I am not in love, Mother Hattie. That would be utterly ridiculous. What I meant to say was; I am in deep like." She stopped as Mother Hattie began to chuckle softly. "I'm so confused." Rayna put her head down on the table.

"I tell you what ridiculous, little Boston baked bean is, it's denying the power of love. You look to me like you're a solid woman. You don't waver to the materialistic offering of a man. Mother Hattie knows some things. And I know you're in love, young one." Mother Hattie leaned her head to the side. "In what ways do you find yourself thinking about him?

Rayna shook her head. "I'm afraid I don't understand the question."

Arching her graying brows, Mother Hattie perched her lips. "Youth is wasted on the young." She looked at Rayna long and hard. Rayna wanted to fidget, but held her ground under the intense probe.

"When you think about him, little innocent one, do you see the both of you doing activities as a couple?" Mother Hattie waved her hand in a circle. "Uh, for instance, like going to church together, taking in a movie, having dinner, or meeting his family one day...couple things. Future established things. Like marriage." Tilting her head slightly, Mother Hattie leaned back waiting, her eyes missing nothing.

"Uh?" Rayna smiled widely.

She realized the road to take with Mother Hattie was one of honesty. Rayna found that she was ready to be transparent with Mother Hattie. She glanced out the huge window, finally allowing her thoughts to roam freely.

"I do think about a couple of things with this man. I see us taking nice walks along the beach." Rayna looked out the window, her voice taking on a dream like quality. "I see us attending morning worship together. I see...," she suddenly stopped.

"Yes?" Mother Hattie asked.

"Nothing, this is ridiculously typical of me. He has probably forgotten all about me. Probably married with two kids and has a dog name Earl." Rayna sucked her teeth in disgust. "Women are always pinning away after small things, oftentimes seeing things that is not there." Rayna cut the air with her hand. "Well, I refuse to be one of those women." She knew she was ranting but couldn't help herself. It felt good to release all the pent up emotions inside of her.

Mother Hattie just smiled. "I see. One more thing, little onion ring. True love exceeds wanting, it is a need."

Rayna took note of the way Mother Hattie emphasized the word true. For the second time that night, she rested her head on the table.

"I need to hear his voice, Mother Hattie. I need to see him. I need to know if he is all right. I need to know what his likes and dislikes are...I need... I don't know. I need something!"

"Calm down, calm down. What you need is a good man in your life. You're wound up tighter than my yarn at home. You need to be unwound, my doll baby." Mother Hattie sipped from her beverage.

"Mother Hattie!" Rayna couldn't help but to laugh.

"Like I said, I ain't been saved all my life. Besides, God didn't intend for man to be alone. I was married to the love of my life. Felix, God bless the dead, was his name. We were married for over thirty years, but that's another story for another time. Look outside."

Rayna glanced out the window. The rain had stopped. She loved how it looked after the rain. Everything seemed so refreshed and renewed. She drew in her breath.

"Mother Hattie, there is something about this man that awakens something inside of here," Rayna pointed to her heart, "which is silly and makes no sense. I feel like one of those female characters in a romance novel. But there is something he's holding back from me. I don't know."

"Stop trying to figure things out. Some things just work themselves out. You'll see. If this man is for you, he will go all the way around the world and come back to you," Mother Hattie said.

Rayna allowed Mother Hattie's words to seep into her heart. Silently, she offered up a prayer of guidance. She didn't know what to do. Her heart wanted to open up and allow love to happen, but her mind wouldn't allow her to forget her flaws.

She smiled at Mother Hattie, concluding to stop worrying about something that may never happen. She was happy with her life. She had a wonderful job, friends and family who loved her, and that was what matter the most.

Chapter 25

"We have to move now. Someone else is in here with us," Sheila said to Monica.

"One two, daddy's coming for you. Three four, never run no more. Five six, no more tricks. Seven eight, my throne I'll take." His voice was closer now. "Nine ten, this battle I'll win." The evil one let loose a sound meant for laughter, but sounded like a wheeze.

Sheila was certain it was the man she seen earlier out her window with the spitting problem.

"Your luck has now run out, little one. I told you there would be nowhere you could go that I would not find you. Our time to rule this world has come. Zion is at hand. These pathetic worshippers of the Nazarene one will see that. Those who will not follow Zion will all perish." His voice was getting closer. "For so many years, the speculation was about the coming again of 'The One; good and evil, dark and light." Again, the wheezing laughter sounded throughout the small cavern. Even the rodents had grown silent.

"The light of love is fading. The world has become infected by greed and selfishness. For so long, the pretenders have ruled this place, but no more. Diseases and decay have caused an unbalance, and it is up to us, The New World Order, to correct this wrong. It will take time and patience, but we are well able."

Sheila helped Monica to her feet. The baby began to cry, and Monica immediately began to breast feed her. Sheila retrieved the old backpack, leading Monica and her newborn further down the small passageway.

"What do I hear? Is that the sound of a newborn baby? You've delivered the promised child. You're making this harder than it needs to be. Come to me, and I promise not to hurt the both of you. You've caused me quite a bit of disturbance, and you must be punished and disciplined. You and your little running mate there. I'm sure by now, you've told her about Zion," the evil one said into the darkness.

LOVE FOUND ME

The acrid smell of smoke was making breathing difficult, and the baby was beginning to whimper, and Sheila she was certain a full outcry was next. She had to do something. Someone had to survive the night.

"Listen, Monica, continue straight ahead. Once you get to the end, on your left there will be a number pad. Key in the number 72509, this will open the hidden door," Sheila said.

Monica refused to move. The baby was becoming more agitated from the smoke. Her cry was like a humming device.

"Don't try to be a hero, Sheila. You have no idea what kind of monster that man is back there." Monica began to shake uncontrollably.

Sheila reached for the baby, fearful that Monica would drop her.

"He is sick and there is no reasoning with him," Monica said.

The baby let forth a loud cry. Both Sheila and Monica turned at the sound of maniacal laughter. He was close. Sheila wanted desperately to leave with Monica and the baby, but knew together they'd never survive. This was the only option.

Again, Mike's beloved face passed before Sheila's eyes. She smiled this time. A familiar passage came to mind. *It was better to have lost love then not to have loved at all.* She understood that now. She understood a lot of things now. She only hoped it wasn't too late to change some things in her life.

She was born for a purpose. Her helping at the women's clinic was not just for her precious babies. It was for her too. She was not only helping them, she was helping herself. She was each one of those women that fell and got back up again. It was fitting that her last moment would be in helping one of her babies out, and she was at peace with it.

"We don't have time for this. I'm giving you and your baby time to get out of here. If you… when you get out, please get help. This is the only way, Monica, and you know it. Now go!" Monica hugged Sheila, tears cascading down her cheeks. Pulling apart Sheila softened the command. "Go."

Swallowing hard, Monica nodded, hugging her baby close, she limped off. Turning, Sheila looked into the eyes of hell. Her time had run out. One hand shot out around her neck, cutting off her air. She tried prying his hands from around her neck, but they remained unmoving. She saw black dots forming behind her eyes.

"Well, well, well. What have we here, a little kitty? It looks like your nine lives are up." Slamming Sheila forcefully against the wall, he leaned in close, closing his eyes, inhaling sharply. "I can smell your fear, breeder."

Sheila's stomach immediately rebelled against his putrid breath. He had wads of spit coursing down his mouth, but it was his words that made her blood go cold. Breeder. Her mind struggled to recall where she heard that term used before.

The dark one opened his eyes, letting them roam over her face. He seemed familiar to her somehow. The question must have shown on her face, for he suddenly smiled. He flung her to the other side of the wall. A loud cracking sound reverberated in the air.

Blinding pain to her head caused Sheila to cry out. She felt something sticky fall in her eyes. She knew if she touched the substance, her hand would draw away blood. Another flash flickered in the back of her mind. This scene seemed familiar to her. She began to slowly crawl, trying in vain to escape her capturer.

"We would have found you eventually, you know. She led us to you sooner, and for that, I won't hurt her too much," the evil one said.

"Who are you? I don't understand," Sheila said.

"Of course you don't understand, but eventually you will. As for whom I am, I'm your leader of the New World Order, breeder. The time to favor Zion is now. I will finally rise up and rule. This place, this world, is rotten from the inside out. These servants of the lesser God, the Nazarene, will all bow to me in submission and reverence."

Sheila crawled up against the wall. Breathing hard, she shoved her hair out of her face. Nazarene? Breeder? He was mad.

"The Nazarene has failed you. He has failed you all. You all are awaiting his return in vain."

"I don't understand what you are talking about. Why are you doing this?" Sheila asked.

"Don't you remember little one?"

Sheila was startled by the question. It was triggering something long ago hidden inside of her. The answer was close, she could tell. But when she tried to reach for it, it evaded her. She saw images. Her head was hurting so bad she couldn't think. Closing her eyes tightly, she began to vomit.

"You are just like your mother...weak." Those words, she heard those words before.

Sheila gasped out loud. She forced herself to look closely at the man. Her eyes widened with recognition. It couldn't be!

He spread his hands out and smiled. "I'm back." Then it happened, all the memories resurfacing then.

Sheila saw images flashing before her; it was like a jigsaw puzzle. The pieces were scattered, needing to be fitted together. Screaming, she grabbed her head and began rocking back and forth against the hard wall. She was oblivious to the rocks cutting into her flesh. She was in another place, another time. There were men wearing masks. They broke into her home, hurting her and her mother; the voice telling her what to do. She had not heard from the voice since that ill-fated night. The whole night had been blotched from her memory until now.

"You are still pathetic." He retrieved a small kerchief from his breast pocket, swiping at the dribble that was his constant companion. He tilted his head to the side and smiled. "This is where I tell you why I did what I did."

Sheila shook her head, not wanting to hear what he had to say. She felt bile rising to her throat.

"Don't!" she screamed.

"Aww, don't you want to know, kitty cat? It's quite an intrigue. I thought that after all these years; you'd want to know the missing pieces of your life. You lost so much blood that night. I honestly believed you wouldn't make it, but you survived. I named you and your sister kitty cats. For the many lives you two have." The man chuckled, as if he just told a funny joke.

The memories came. They were sharp and clear. She felt like she was actually transported back into the past. She was ten years old again. She rolled to her knees, as her stomach emptied itself. The pieces were finally coming together; the intruders brutally attacking her mother.

The voice! She remembered the voice. It had not spoken to her since that ill fated night. The voice had warned her of danger that night. She wasn't crazy. Maybe it was some type of inherited six-sense or gift. She and Monica were sisters and both experienced hearing the inner voice.

The dark one spit on the ground next to her foot.

"Bumbling idiot, he couldn't even complete the assignment given him. His incompetence put back my timing on becoming Zion's new leader." Slowly, he walked to Sheila. Crouching down until he was eye level, he captured her chin, forcing her to look at him.

"Your father failed. He was supposed to teach you the way of Zion. You are one of the many that were to produce the New World Order. The coward got greedy, took off with my money. For that, he had to pay. No one disobeys my orders, and they certainly don't steal from me. There is no place on this earth that I cannot find you. We are many, and we grow strong everyday. You are a breeder, one of many. The chosen ones."

Sheila whimpered. This had to be a dream, one big horrible dream. A thing like this doesn't happen in the real world. Something triggered in her mind. She stopped rocking, the final pieces coming together.

She had passed out and woke up in the hospital. She had received severe head trauma, and was in ICU for over a month. She had no relatives, so she became a ward of the state. She was placed in a foster home, and was cared for by a wonderful couple until she was eighteen years of age. She then went to college, and after graduation is when she began working for The Mending Heart.

She looked at the man from her past; a man whom she'd grown to hate. Because of him, her mother was dead. Because of him, she was the basket case she was today. She was suddenly mad. No, she was angry. The loss of her mother, the loss of her innocence came flooding back to her. She was tired of being the victim. She was determined to be the victor, and if she had to die to be that, then so be it.

Chapter 26

Mike's heart slammed hard against his rib cage at the heavy amount of smoke coming from Sheila's house. He immediately exited his car, and was about to run into the house when strong arms caught him.

Without hesitation, he went into combat mode. He sent a quick left, but it was immediately blocked. Mike went low, kicking his assailant's feet from under him. The man landed on his back, and immediately kicked forward, coming up on his feet landing in warrior position. Mike attempted to do an up kick, but was stopped; upon hearing a familiar voice.

"Chill man, it's me, Eric."

"Eric?" Mike questioned. Eric was wearing his signature all black; it was hard to recognize him in the fading light.

"She might not be in there." Eric clasped Mike on the shoulder in greeting.

Mike swallowed hard, and could only nod in response. "My gut instincts are telling me that she's in that burning inferno somewhere, man," he said. From the corner of his eye, Mike caught a movement. "Look over there." He pointed in the direction in which the movement came from.

They looked at each other briefly before simultaneously running in the direction they saw the object fall. Mike's heart dropped when he saw the body on the ground. It took a moment for the sound of a baby crying to register with him. Eric had already reached the fallen body.

"It's a woman and baby." Eric rolled the woman over, allowing his hands to search for broken bones. He then reached for the baby, who was crying loudly. He was relieved that there were no broken bones.

"That's the girl from the shelter Sheila was trying to protect," Mike said. Kneeling down beside the woman, he questioned her. "Where is Sheila?" His voice sound strained.

LOVE FOUND ME

Eric went rigid. He looked at the house engulfed in flames. It didn't look good. Beside him, the woman was murmuring something softly. Eric stood, reaching inside his jacket, retrieving his cell.

"This is Detective Wade, requesting backup and an ambulance, and fire truck stat at 215 Benson Lane. We have a mother and a newborn in need of medical assistant. A house is on fire, and a possible homicide. Again, requesting 10-13, 10-47 and 10-50; back up, an ambulance and fire assistance." Eric shut his cell phone. He looked around and noticed Mike was gone. He started to run after Mike, but the woman began to cough.

"Help her, please. Sheila, my sister, needs help. He is going to kill her," Monica cried.

"Who is going to kill her?" Eric eased her head onto his lap.

Monica worked her mouth, but began coughing viciously from hailing in too much smoke. She passed out before Eric could ask her any further questions. Eric picked up the crying baby into his arms and did something he hadn't done in years. He prayed.

* * *

Mike followed the directions Monica had given him as to where Sheila was. He saw the door. To the left was a small keypad. He punched in the numbers Monica hastily supplied to him. He had just entered the small passageway, and immediately became drenched with sweat. The heat was almost intolerable, it was sheer will and determination that kept him going. For a moment, he felt himself panicking. His breathing was becoming labored, and his heart felt like it was going to explode. He shook his head to clear it. He got lower on the ground, desperately trying to breath in fresh air. It helped, but slowed down his progress. It was once again that he allowed his mind to return to the night of the accident.

He could never say his wife's name before, but the need to say it aloud was strong. Hurt was causing him to feel sick to the stomach. Swallowing hard, he began crawling faster as if trying to outrun the painful memories.

His wife's name was Tiffany. His heart lurched then settled back. Mike smiled as he remembered their brief time together; their confessions to each other, their family planning, and their childhood memories. It all came back to him. He began laughing aloud, recalling one memory of Tiffany putting a frog down his shirt in retribution.

He had forgotten he had made plans with her to go fishing. Instead, he went with Bryan to his friend's house to watch a football game. Suffice it to say, he never broke their engagements again. He thought he would be feeling guilty, but suddenly felt inward warmth washing over him.   Looking up, he thought he saw his wife holding an infant in her arms. He and Tiffany were going to name their daughter Hannah. Mike stopped. Blinking several times, certain his mind was playing tricks on him. Tiffany smiled and pushed back the pink blanket covering the infant. The baby began squirming, her chubby legs kicking in and out. On her mop of curly tresses was a small pink bow.

The baby suddenly turned, holding Mike's stare. She looked like a combination of both him and his wife. Her eyes were a light brown, like her mother's. Her chin was that of the Montgomery's, like his. Mike's throat restricted more. Their image was beginning to glow bright, and he had to cover his eyes because the light was so bright.

When he looked up again, his wife and daughter was no longer there. Mike didn't know what to believe anymore. Had he imagined what just happened? He was suddenly afraid he was going mad. Things like this didn't happen in the real world.

Keep going. You don't have much time. Mike looked around the small tunnel. There was no one there. *Get up, you are needed.* He was paralyzed by doubt. Tiffany, young and talented, she had so much to give the world. So many things left undone. He wept for his unborn child, who never had the opportunity to see the light of day.

LOVE FOUND ME

Mike began to crawl faster; the rocks were embedding themselves in his hands and knees. He stopped crawling, suddenly collapsing onto the hard ground. *You have to keep going, don't give up now.* He once again looked around the little small passage.

He was confident no one was there, yet he tangibly heard a voice speaking to him. *Why do people always doubt me? They seek me, and when I answer, it is hard for them to believe that I am with them. It is easy to believe they are crazy than to believe that I truly exist. Mike, I never left you or your wife.* Mike hit the ground hard with his fist at the mention of Tiffany's name. *You have been forgiven, Mike. You are released from the burdens of the past. It is up to you to release them and never pick them up again. Your future is brighter than your past. Get up and live.*

Mike remembered once feeling that he never heard God's voice. Was this God speaking to him? He felt a warmth coursing through him. Suddenly feeling renewed, he stood up on his feet. His mission was to find his love…Sheila.

* * *

Eric looked up and saw three figures clad in dark robes were exiting the burning building. They were heading toward a dark car. When the tallest of the group stopped, he pointed in Eric's direction. He and one of the goons began walking toward him. The third one stood back a distance. Eric gently placed the woman on the ground.

Monica grabbed his arm. "Please don't leave me and my baby," she pleaded.

Eric smiled. "I'm not going to let any harm come to you or your baby." He watched as Monica's eyes traveled over his face. She nodded. Standing slowly, he moved away from her and her child. "Trick or treating early, fellas?" he asked the men.

The two men began to circle around Eric, as if looking for an opening. Eric was ready for the attack. It came from the taller man. Eric nimbly stepped aside, karate kicking the man from behind. He landed hard on the pavement unconscious.

The second man ran to Eric, and again Eric stepped to the side, evading his punch. Eric went low, punching him first in the stomach, and then landing a series of rights to his face. It wasn't long before he too joined his partner on the pavement.

Eric looked around for the third man, but he had disappeared. Eric heard the sound of sirens in the distance. At last, back up was close. He couldn't go into the house until they arrived taking his unconscious burdens into custody. He was concerned about the third man.

Chapter 27

Sheila stopped rocking. The man's eyes widened in surprise.

"Well, well. Maybe I've underestimated you after all, kitty cat. Maybe I should call you lioness," the man said.

"You are crazy. I'm a human being with feelings. I'm not anyone's breeding machine. You think you're going to get away with capturing women and forcing them to have children. What is in the dark always comes to the light."

He just laughed, walking around in the small tunnel. He reminded her of a restless panther.

"I've heard all that chicken scratch before, girly. You think the pathetic judicial system scares me? Everyone has a price. How do you think I was able to find you?"

"You are sick. You will never get away with this. I have someone who loves me, and will stop at nothing to find me." Sheila stopped, noting that his eyes had grown darker. She resisted the urge to look down as she had done when she was a child. She raised her chin in defiance, refusing to bow down.

"Yes, I know of who you speak. He is weak. He couldn't protect his wife and unborn child, and now it seems he can't protect you." Sheila gasped. "He was a hindrance to us; to Zion. The baby she carried belonged to the New World Order. She shouldn't have resisted. Nothing good can come from resisting us. Tiffany was to be my wife, breeder of my children, but she left, fancying herself to have found true love." He laughed, the evil sound bouncing off the wall. He again swiped at the saliva. "She tried valiantly to protect him, so she bargained her child's life for his life. She was to have the child and give him to us for her and Mike's chance at happiness. But silly, silly girl broke the rules. She was preparing to leave town with her baby and her lover boy." The dark one squatted down in front of Sheila. "I am one man you don't lie to. So she had to be punished."

"You've always talked too much," a voice came from behind.

The man spun around. Sheila watched a man in a dark robe walk further into the room and stand directly in front of her. She gasped in shock when he pulled the hood back off his head. The evil one smiled.

"Bartholomew, how nice of you to finally join us after all these years." He stood up, shifting his weight from foot to foot. The air grew heavy with the combination of smoke and fear. "So the chicken has come home to roost." He looked at Sheila and grinned. "Well, let's get this father-daughter reunion over with. As you can see we don't have much time." The smoke was becoming thicker, and the heat was making it difficult to breathe.

Sheila recognized the popped eyes belonging to her father. He held her stare. There was something about his eyes that seemed different.

"I have a lot to make up for. I don't blame you if you never forgive me. I certainly know that I'm not deserving of it. However, please forgive me for treating you and your mother like cattle."

Sheila could only stare wide-eyed at the man who made her life a living hell. The fact that he was asking for forgiveness was ludicrous.

"I have seen the light, Sheila. I now know what I did was wrong. That night, I went to a bar and got drunk. I browned out. When I came through, later that night, I saw your mother's broken body. There was no help for her. I saw that you were alive, barely. I picked you up and drove you to the hospital. You were in the ICU for days. I stayed there until you came out of a coma. I knew that I couldn't stay with you, because I would be a danger to you. I called a friend of mine who worked at a foster home, and asked them to take care of you. I gave them monthly payments from your trust fund that your mother opened for you. Your mother didn't think I knew about it. You are wealthy, Sheila. He bent down, producing a well-worn envelope. This will explain everything."

LOVE FOUND ME

Sheila could only listen; she had no more tears to shed. She had suddenly grown numb. She looked at the envelope in her father's outstretched hand. He finally let it fall into her lap. She looked up into eyes, familiar, yet different. They were sorrowful.

"When your mother died, it felt like something died inside of me. I was empty and started feeling depressed. The organization just wasn't the same. It felt wrong somehow. One night, I was sleeping and this bright light surrounded me. I saw myself for what I was, a wretch. That night, I asked whoever, whatever that was, to please forgive me."

"And now, you want me to forgive you just like that? Some light surrounds you, and now you're seeking freedom from your guilt. Well, you can wait until the sky turns purple. My mother is dead because of you!" Sheila said.

The dark one began to laugh, as if she had told a joke. Sheila sent him a scathing look. She had almost forgotten about him. He simply smiled, raising both brows in humor.

Her father didn't deny her accusation. He bowed his head. "Your words are true. I am cursed to carry with me that burden for the rest of my life," her father said.

"Oh, Bartholomew, you've always had a flare for the dramatics. Her mother would have died eventually anyway. The weak ones always do. In this world, it's the survival of the fittest. Anyways, I'm growing bored with this. You did what we told you to do. Now, you found the light and have deviated from the plan, and for that, you too must be extinguished."

"I will do so willingly, but I will not let you harm my daughter."

"You don't have a say in the matter, you pathetic coward. Consider yourself eradicated. You're a dead man walking. Maybe in the place beyond, you'll seek the reprieve you're longing for, I mean that." He pulled out a long wicked knife, advancing on Bartholomew.

"You can't hurt me anymore than I have been hurting these past years. I'm tormented daily. I can't sleep. Every time I close my eyes, I see the face of the one woman I loved. I have asked God to forgive me years ago, and although He may have forgiven me, in the end it is I who can't forgive myself."

The dark one was getting closer to her father, the knife still in his hand. Her father just stood there like the proverbial sheep, ready to be sacrificed. Her father looked at Sheila and mouthed the words *forgive me.*

"Wait! Don't hurt him. I will do what you ask, please no more killings," Sheila said.

The dark one turned to look at Sheila. "Oh, my dear, just one more time," he said.

Her father lunged at the man, struggling to gain possession of the knife. "Run, Sheila, get out now!"

Sheila scrambled to her feet, preparing to run. She heard a loud gasping sound. Turning, she saw her father crumpling to the floor. She ran to him.

"Why didn't you leave, child? Don't make my sacrifice in vain," he moaned.

"I couldn't leave you again," she said.

He began to cough, blood streaming from the side of his mouth. He reached out his hand; Sheila took it without hesitation. "I truly am sorry for the hurt I caused you and your mother. I was blinded by the lies and greed. I ask that you forgive me." He began coughing up more blood. Sheila could feel his hands getting cold, an indication that he hadn't much time left. "Also, I ask that you release me. Release the hurt I done to you. You deserve complete happiness, baby girl. None of this today is your fault, never was. Evil is to blame. Understand me. Evil is to blame." Sheila nodded, blinded by her tears.   "Good girl."

"Daddy?" Her father looked at her. "I forgive you. I release you."

He said nothing, just looked at her. His eyes began to well up with tears; they fell like rain drops falling off a windowpane. He nodded his head, and taking a last breath, he smiled. Sheila folded his hands across his chest and smiled back. She should have felt overwhelming sorrow, but instead she felt at peace, as if a missing part of her was filled.

"I hate sappy endings." The dark one was leaning casually against the wall, not bothering to wipe the blood dripping from the knife off. "It's time to go, breeder. Let the dead bury the dead."

* * *

Eric stood when he heard the sirens approaching. At last, it seemed like an eternity since he'd placed the call for help. The ambulance was the first to arrive on the scene, then came Atlanta's finest. Eric stepped aside, allowing the paramedics to do their job.

Monica reached out her hand, stopping him from leaving. "Please, you've got to help my sister," she pleaded. "There's a secret passage around the back of the house." Eric listened as she called off the code number to him. She affirmed his suspicions regarding Mike's disappearance. She had given Mike the same directions and password. Eric motioned for the police officers to follow him. They took off in the direction that Monica gave him.

* * *

Sheila's eyes widened with joy, her actions revealing Mike's presence. She couldn't help it; he was her light in that dark moment. The evil one swirled around, only to be forcefully penned to the wall by Mike.

"Oh great, just when I thought it was safe to make my grand exit, a little boy comes along." The deviant began to laugh riotously.

"Sheila, baby, are you okay?" Mike demanded, not daring to take his eyes off the man. Mike slammed the man hard against the wall twice.

Sheila ran her hands through her hair. "Yes, I'm fine." She looked around for the envelope. Finding it, she stuffed it into her back pants pocket.

"You don't know what you've gotten yourself into, boy. We are many and you are few. The best thing for you to do is to turn around and leave the same way came. The breeder belongs to me."

Mike was tired; he was in no mood to hear trash talking from some maniac. The fact he dared touch his lady sealed his fate. All he wanted to do was hold Sheila in his arms and make sure she was truly all right.

Mike looked imposing to Sheila. It was obvious, he was passed being angry. He was furious. Her heart accelerated when she realized it was all on her behalf. If she hadn't known before then, she definitely knew it now. Mike loved her! She wanted desperately to run to him, to feel his arms around her in comfort.

"I haven't been a boy in years, old man. Sheila belongs to God first, and I second. No where do you fit in the equation." Mike leaned in close, lowering his voice, raw emotions causing his eyes to darken. The man began to laugh loudly, spit flying everywhere. Mike was repulsed by the display.

"Join us. Join our crusade." The man began to scowl, nostrils flaring. "Zion will rise up and take over the world. We are the true people of the world. The prophecy is going to be fulfilled, and you cannot stop it. Join us, boy."

Sheila softly whimpered. Mike shook his head; slamming the man hard against the wall again. The stranger yelled out loud, and then laughed eerily.

"You've got a dark side, boy. I like that. Everyone has a dark side. Tell me, what it would take to get you to crossover?" the dark one said.

Mike began to doubt himself again. Could that be the reason why his wife and child were killed, because of some evil stain inside of him? Was that the reason why he never really heard from God? What about the voice he heard moments ago? How could he be certain that the voice wasn't some evil entity influencing his actions?

"Mike, don't listen to him. There is nothing dark about you. You are my light. I couldn't see until you came into my life. Your love for me caused the sun to shine for me," Sheila said.

Her voice was like a balm to his tumultuous thoughts. She was his anchor. She was pulling him back from that dark place of the past. There he felt less of a man. There he was a failure. What if he failed Sheila like, he failed his wife and unborn child? Was there some kind of evil in him that this dark one recognized? The thought was sickening. He was not dark or evil. He was sure Sheila would recognize it if he were. Where there is light, darkness cannot tarry. Sheila was definitely the light. Mike shook his head.

"You caught me at a good moment. Years ago, had I met you, then you would no longer be in existence." Mike reared back his first hitting him, rendering the dark one unconscious.

At last, Sheila ran to him and he caught her. She clung to him as if she never would let him go.

"Mike, I thought I would never see you again. There is so much I need to say to you." Sheila cupped Mike's face with her hands. Her words were coming out rushed and disoriented, but she didn't care. She was just happy to be in the arms of the man she loved.

Mike said nothing, he just continued to hold her, she was rambling on and on, and he let her. He heard someone coming from behind. Turning, he saw it was Eric and some uniformed police officers. Eric nodded at Mike.

"We have to roll, man. This house is ready to give at any moment," Eric said.

Mike lifted Sheila up into his arms. "Her attacker is by the wall."

"Did you have to kill him, man?" Eric questioned.

Mike turned in confusion. "I didn't kill him." He looked where the body of the dark one should have been. He was gone.

"He is gone," Sheila voiced his thoughts. Mike felt her shudder and squeezed her tight. "That is the body of my father. Mike didn't kill him. The evil one did."

With that, Mike turned and walked out the small corridor, anxious to take care of his true love. He would let Eric and the uniforms handle the body.

Epilogue

The art gallery was packed, courtesy of the media. The story was about an up and coming artist who had thwarted death, from what was allegedly hailed as a serial killer, and who was a part of secret society, was a reporters delight. The harrowing ordeal had made the local and national headlines. The harrowing ordeal had made the local and national headlines.

Mike thought Sheila looked beautiful. She was wearing a long red dress that accentuated her curves modestly. On her neck were two layered pearls. She had her hair up in a coif. Her eyes were bright with joy.

It had been two months since her father's death. Two months of her crying, and two months of Mike trying to persuade her to be his wife. When she finally said yes, he felt like he was on top of the world.

The wedding was set to take place in three weeks, and he was more than ready for Sheila to take on his last name. He wanted to watch the sun set and rise with her for the rest of their lives.

"A penny for your thoughts?" Mike looked down into the most beautiful eyes in the world. They were on the dance floor waltzing. He could feel the stares of his family and friends watching them. He knew what they saw...true love.

"I was just thinking how blessed I am to have you in my life." Mike leaned in closer to Sheila, inhaling her essence. "I love you, Sheila, with all my heart. I'm going to spend the rest of my life making you happy. With God on my side, I can do it. I almost lost you, baby." He hugged her close to him. His embrace was almost painful, but Sheila didn't mind, she hugged him back just as fiercely.

"I love you too, Mike. God, in His own unique way, has given us both a second chance at love. I'm going to take full advantage of it." Sheila looked in the direction of her best friend. She was sitting next to Eric; there was a frown on both of their faces. "I have a feeling there is something going on between Rayna and Eric," she said.

Mike didn't bother to look up; he was too focused on Sheila. She felt good in his arms. He would worry about their friends later. He had a feeling everything was going to be all right.

He remembered the voice in the small corridor when he was trying to get to Sheila. He was happy. He thought of how Sheila had saved her sister, Monica, and her baby. Monica was still in a safe house with her baby, Miracle. She was content to be there as long as she needed to be. She was just happy that she and her baby were safe.

There was still no trace of Sheila's attacker. Mike didn't have a name for him. In mutual agreement they resorted in calling him the dark one. He was out there waiting, but Mike was ready for him. The dark one's time was limited. Eric was confident he would one day find him. In fact, seeking the evil one out is the bulk of where his time went. Eric was afraid the dark one would link Rayna also in his evil plan.

He finally glanced up at his friend. Sheila was right, Eric didn't look too happy. Rayna was no longer sitting beside him. She was on the dance floor with a man Mike recognized from his church. He knew for a fact he was single and very successful. Eric was in for the fight of his life and his heart. Mike smiled, hugging Sheila closer to him. Eric was in for the fight of his life and his heart. He couldn't wait to see how his friend handles finding a true love of his own.

Coming in 2010 in the "Love Series"
Eric Miller and Rayna Peterson Story

VANESSA RICHARDSON

About the Author

Vanessa Richardson is an author, poet, and playwright. Vanessa has written several stage productions and has been blessed to perform them at various venues. Her stage production includes

"Mama Rainey"
"Someone To Love Me"
"Why Do Bad Things Happens To Good People?"
"Lord, I Don't Understand"
"The Fullness Of Time"

Vanessa wrote her freshman inspirational novel, *"The Certain Ones"* a spiritual impacting novel that inspires her readers to know that not everyone are called into greatness. *Fact: Many cannot handle the process that goes along with becoming great. Only the certain ones that endure can obtain greatness.* Vanessa is currently working on her second fiction novel titled, *"Love Lifted Me"*

"When a man's ways please the LORD, He maketh even his enemies to be at peace with him." (Proverbs 16:7)

LOVE FOUND ME

GSH Publishing
Book Order Form

Please (√) your novel(s) of interest

___ *Love Found Me* by Vanessa Richardson
$15.00+$3.99 s/h

___ *Drama* by George Hudson
$10.00+$3.99 s/h

___ *A Mother's Cry* by Elva "Precious Love" Thompson
$15.00+$3.99 s/h

___ *Rhythm Can't Keep Time* by Deondriea Cantrice
$15.00+$3.99 s/h

___ *What We Won't Do For Love* by Ms. Robinson
$15.00+$3.99 s/h

Please Print Clearly

First Name: _____

Last Name: _____

Mailing Address: _____

City / State / Zip: _____

Telephone:_____

E-mail: _____

Make money orders and/or institutional checks payable to:

GSH Publishing
P.O. Box 350646
Palm Coast, FL 32135
www.gshpublishing.com